The Spycatcher Caper

The Spycatcher Caper

Robert Muccigrosso

Acknowledgments

My love and gratitude go to my wife, Maxine, who read the manuscript, offered valuable suggestions, and provided the nourishing surroundings that have made work possible. I also once more wish to thank Mitchell Phillips and Rosalie Bruce for their ongoing friendship and support. Rosalie deserves my special gratitude for the technical assistance that helped to shape the manuscript into a book.

Finally, my thanks go to PhilipsInc for providing the cover for this book.

For Maxine
and
In memory of my parents, Egidia and Henry Muccigrosso

Chapter 1

I'm proud to serve my country and can't wait to kill some lousy Krauts and Nips and whoever else is lousy."

Standing tall (although he was not of noteworthy height) before the Selective Service System draft board, the gumshoe wanted the board's members to know that when duty called, as it was now loudly doing, he was all ears. He was all courage. He was all-American. He was the real thing. He was... And the fact that he had failed to respond to the initial three letters the board had sent was clearly due to a misunderstanding.

The weary retired major who chaired the board cut him short. "Yes, Mr. De-Witt, you've shown us your good faith. And now it's time that you show your good faith and fighting spirit to the military. As soon as you pass your physical examination, you'll shortly be receiving orders as to where and when to report. And by the way," the colonel smiled, "I think we can forget the little mix-up that could have sent you to prison at Fort Leavenworth." DeWitt thanked him, saluted nervously and needlessly, and left the room without looking back. "That was a close one," he told himself. "I could have spent my life in a military shithole prison. Now

all I got to worry about is keeping my life until this shit war ends."

What the private eye had told the board was true. Well, mostly. Well, a little. He did hate his country's enemies and he had been prepared to fight the war–but looking on from the sidelines. After all, every fighting man, he reasoned, needed cheerleaders to boost his morale.

The war had been raging for more than a year after Pearl Harbor when Dick DeWitt, who had been a private investigator for nearly twenty years, had received the notice from his draft board to report for a physical examination. This surprised him. Though without wife or child, he was in his early forties, too old, he figured, to sling an M-16 over his left shoulder and hunt for the nation's enemies. The unpleasant news demanded a shot of Jack Daniel's, and then a second and a third, after which he stumbled into bed and bid the problem good night until the morning.

Five days intervened before his scheduled physical, and DeWitt spent much of his time and thought (detractors had long snickered that he had little of the latter) working on how he could beat the system. Appearance, he reckoned, counted, and so he deprived himself of shaving, bathing, and changing underwear, arriving at the large physical examination center to the disgusted looks and disbelief of both fellow examinees and examiners. "Hey, pal, you know how bad you stink?" asked one young fellow sporting a pronounced Brooklyn accent. DeWitt made strange noises in response, not because he failed to have understood the question but due to his plan to display a speech impediment to the examiners.

"Next," yelled a tough-looking soldier whose three stripes denoted the rank of sergeant. "Yeah, you, stinky. Haul your smelly ass over to Table 3, and be quick about it."

DeWitt dutifully limped to Table 3 and commenced to mumble incoherently. The doctor stared and then announced to the physician at the adjoining table, "I've got a live one here, John. Do you want him?" John apparently did not, since he shook his head and clamped two fingers to his nostrils.

"All right, Mr... He leafed through a few sheets of typewritten pages. "All right, Mr. DeWhite, I'd like for you to tell me about any maladies, conditions, or problems you may have that would keep you from the company of Uncle Sam's forces."

"Speak up, Mr. DeWhite, I can't understand what you're saying."

After thirty seconds or so of DeWitt's mumbling, the doctor, annoyed but finding it difficult to suppress a smile, ordered the private eye to write down what he was trying to convey.

DeWitt considered shrugging his shoulders as if to indicate that he was illiterate but feared that the ploy might be pushing it too far. Instead, he scribbled a list of encumbrances that might have brought tears to the eyes of the compassionate, of whom, he hoped, the doctor sitting across the table was one. DeWitt first listed flat feet and hoped that the bedroom slippers he was wearing would provide sufficient proof. Then there was his left knee, which he claimed he had severely injured while saving a young woman from the clutches of a sex fiend. (DeWitt, in fact, had injured his knee—but not too severely—while jumping out of a second-story window to avoid the return of an unsuspecting husband.) Hemorrhoids, he added, kept him from sitting for more than a quarter of an hour. If he sat longer, he farted uncontrollably. Finally, there was the matter of the index finger, or, rather, both of them. As a private detective, he had badly injured them when a notorious jewel thief, whom he had caught in the act, viciously slammed the door of a safe on those precious digits need to fire a rifle. (In truth, the only time he had injured his index fingers came as he was trying to unhook the bra of his secretary Dotty, who fell heavily backward on him.)

Looking at the list of afflictions, the doctor said that he sympathized with a man who had suffered such misfortunes, but that the man still would have to undergo a physical exam. "Go to the line over there, Mr. DeWhite. And by the way," he added as DeWitt limped away, Dr. Goldfarb will give you a special exam. He's one of the city's most noted urologists. No one knows a prostate better than him."

The doctor had examined DeWitt with few comments and even less display of emotion. Not so Dr. Irving Goldfarb, who plunged right in, so to speak, and elicited a piercing yelp from his victim. "Come on now, soldier. That's no way to act. What are you going to do when the going gets really rough? Besides, you don't want me to do a slipshod exam on something as important as your prostate, do you?" DeWitt muttered something, but this time he was not acting.

"Good news. Your prostrate is as soft as a baby's tushy," Dr. Goldfarb pronounced, "now go down two tables to your right and let Dr. Grosshandler make sure you don't have a hernia."

DeWitt walked gingerly to his next appointment. "I don't know if I have a hernia, Doc, but I get this sharp pain next to my nuts every time I try to lift anything that weighs more than two or three pounds. It's really awful."

"Well let me check you out. Drop your drawers, fellow. Hmm. No initial indication of hernia. No swelling at all. But let's make sure." The doctor placed his hand on the right side of DeWitt's groin. "Okay, now cough for me."

"I can't, Doc. It hurts too much when I cough."

Grosshandler stared at him. "I think we can rule out a hernia. Sometimes the pain you describe stems not from a hernia but from a rare occlusion of certain vessels in the testicles. Here, I'm going to give them a slight twist so that your sperms can swim as nice as Esther Williams. There, that should serve to alleviate the discomfort you experience when you lift anything heavy"

Startled examiners and examinees alike looked at the fortysomething man with his trousers and shorts around his ankles. Most wondered what had caused his screams. A few may have noticed Dr. Grosshandler wink at Dr. Goldfarb and the broad smile that the latter returned.

The ordeal ended after slightly more than two hours with the promise that he would receive official notification of the exam's results within a few days. DeWitt, his prostate and testicles still calling out "Don't do that," dressed, left the building, grabbed an uptown bus, settled into his apartment, thought of having a late morning Jack Daniel's, and acted on the thought.

The letter arrived via special delivery several days later on a hot mid-July early morning. Still groggy from sleep and some libations from the previous evening, DeWitt tore open the envelope, read the letter, and reached for the back of an old kitchen chair to steady himself. "I-A! Holy Toledo! Holy shit!" How could this happen? he wondered. Me, with all my afflictions. Me, who's giving his all to protect women, children, and a few men from the evil that stalks our city. If I join the Army, who'll take care of all these people?

DeWitt's concerns for humanity soon yielded to his concerns for saving his hide. The letter announced that he had fourteen days from the time of receipt to report to a New Jersey fort for induction. Failure to do so would constitute a criminal act and would be subject to the fullest rigors of the military code. "These guys aren't fooling around," the private eye muttered. "Uncle Sam wants me bad."

His Uncle may have lusted after him, but the nephew didn't reciprocate. The only hots the latter had was for his own well-being and for a couple of broads who lived on the West Side. No, he reasoned, it's senseless for me to go to war when there's a war going on in our cities. Sure, Uncle Sam needs help, but so, too, do J. Edgar Hoover and his FBI starched-collared, pressed-pants agents and every other law enforcement officer here in the good old US of A. "I'm needed here!" With no one present in the kitchen to dispute his firm conclusion, the crime fighter turned to the thought of breakfast and perhaps brushing his teeth.

Two slices of Wonder Bread smeared with mayonnaise, some rashers of slightly (but only slightly) moldy bacon, and a few dill pickles, washed down by a cup of Maxwell House put the gumshoe in a better frame of mind to deal with his predicament. Relying on his keen powers and experience, he deduced that he was in one hell of a pickle instead of being, as he not infrequently was, pickled. Two roads, both dark and dangerous, lay open: he could accept induction or he could refuse. Stark opposite courses with no smooth path in between. His emotions, instincts, and thoughts pulled and tugged, ending in snarls that a glass of Jack Daniel's failed to untangle.

DeWitt told himself that he had little time to make the decision that one way or another would alter his life forever, perhaps even take that life. Maybe those who cared for him could offer wise counsel. Trouble was that few people did care for him. Talking it over with a man of the cloth seemed out of the question. He had rarely felt the stirrings of religion, and the last time he had attended church was with a cute librarian who said she could never offer her body to anyone who was not deeply religious. He had told her that he had been an altar boy, but when pressed, he said for a Southern Baptist congregation when he was in his mid-twenties. The librarian stuck to her books and failed to permit him to stick to her body.

Why not turn to Mom? he asked himself. True they had an ambivalent relationship—he loved her, she loathed him—but mothers are mothers, and when the chips are down they can be counted on.

Shortly after breakfast he decided to skip washing the dishes or brushing his teeth and went straight to the heart of the matter.

"Hi, Mom, this is your son, Dick."

"I was afraid so. Whatever you want make it snappy because I got to feed the gold fish."

"It's nice to hear your voice, Mom."

"Cut the crap, sonny boy. Why the hell are you wasting my time? The last time you phoned was to ask if I wanted another can opener for Christmas, and I told you where you could put it. You've given me the same stupid can opener every Christmas since I can remember. And I didn't even drop you on your head when you were a baby, though, Lord knows, I should have."

"Mom, I've got a problem."

"Well, who the hell doesn't? You think you're someone special?"

"But this is really a big one, Mom. The Army wants to draft me… What's so funny, Mom?"

"You know, sonny boy, you just handed me the biggest laugh I've had since your Uncle Jeremiah fell down his cellar steps, broke a leg, an arm, and a hip, and wound up in the hospital for a few months. He never was the same again. Lord, how we all did laugh."

"But, Mom, what should I do about the Army?

"Well, I think you should join up with either the Nazis or the Japs. That way we'd be sure to win the war a lot sooner. That's my advice, sonny boy. Take it or leave it. Now I got to get to the goldfish. One last thing. Wherever you are next Christmas, don't send me another goddamned can opener or I'll find you and give that piece of junk a good shoving you know where."

The war hadn't diminished his mother's sense of humor, Dick thought, but it hadn't helped to resolve his problem, either. After lunch, he called his secretary Dotty, though it was a Saturday and she was at home rather than at their office. He knew that this would be a long shot, since his Gal Friday was Daffy Dotty on any given day of the week. Though she had worked for him for years and served him faithfully, he could not understand how, on the one hand, she could read great works of literature but on the other hand, have the intelligence that ranged between Stan Laurel and Mortimer Snerd. Nevertheless, he reasoned, a would-be draft inductee couldn't be choosy. And just maybe, Daffy Dotty could say something helpful for a change.

"Hi, Dotty, it's Dick."

"Dick who?"

Dotty's boss was tempted to say "Sorry, wrong number," and slam the receiver down. Instead, he said, "This is Dick DeWitt, private investigator. May I please speak with Dorothy Krunchnik?"

"Oh, Mr. D, it's you. Why didn't you say so in the first place? And why are you so formal? Haven't I always been "Dotty" to you?"

You've always been a lot of things to me, Dick thought: occasionally competent secretary, source of more than occasional erections, but most of all, frequent pain in the butt.

"Dotty, I'm sorry I'm bothering you at home on your day off."

"No bother, Mr. D. I was just rereading *The Odyssey*. It's slower going this time around, since I'm reading it in Greek… Hello? Mr. D? You still there?"

"Yes, I'm still here. Now listen, Dotty, I've got a problem that maybe you can help me with. To come right to the point, the Army wants me to serve."

"Oh, Mr. D, that's funny. Doesn't the Army know that you don't know how to serve? Don't you remember the time you fixed your special soup for me on a paper plate and with a ladle? And on top of that, I wound up in the hospital with food poisoning. Oh no, Mr. D, you shouldn't serve in the Army."

It was another pain in the butt time, another occasion to wonder what he saw in this ditzy dame in the first place except for her oversized breasts and cute ass. "Dotty, just shut up for a minute and listen to me." He patiently explained the situation in simplest terms possible. "Now what do you think I should do?"

A substantial pause ensued. "Mr. D, I think you've got a real problem. I'm afraid you're going to lose either way, that's what I think."

Not able to strangle her, DeWitt wanted to fire her on the spot but managed to restrain himself. "Okay, Dotty, thanks."

"No, thank you for giving me the chance to help. By the way, shall I come into work on Monday, or will you have run away by that time? And what if you do run away and get caught and wind up in some dirty prison cell, or you do the right thing and help your country, though you might get wounded or even worse, should I keep watering the flowers in the office? Whatever you decide, Mr. D, I hope that I've cheered you up."

DeWitt had saved his best hope for sage advice for last: Phil ("Polish Phil") Mazurki, a retired decorated policeman known for having collared numerous tough mugs but legendary for having been on the take. The gumshoe had not yet contacted his longtime friend, since the latter was visiting his cousin, Walter, who, though an Illinois state judge, was currently serving a five-year sentence in Joliet Prison for corruption. Phil, he knew, would return to his fancy apartment situated high atop the city's East River. Until then Dick would have to perform some thumb-twiddling.

That evening, thumbs sore from repeated twiddling, he walked to The Slippery Elbow, a local purveyor of suds that for years had served as a home away from home. The Elbow had always attracted his kind of people and his kind of drinks. Sort of, because Gus the barman, when unwatched, watered his drinks as though they were flowers badly in need of rain.

"Whatta you have, deadbeat?" Gus asked as soon as DeWitt entered the grimy premises. "You gonna pay for it or put it on the tab? This way I'll know if you're going to help put food on my kids' plates or let them go hungry." DeWitt chuckled. Only Mom has a better sense of humor than old Gus.

The gumshoe looked around the room to see whose elbows were bent and whose ears he could bend. The years had taken their toll of both moderate drinkers and confirmed lushes. Some had moved on to lusher pastures, so to speak. A few had developed delirium tremens and were residing in Bellevue Hospital or a noted facility on Long Island. The saddest loss of all was that of "Light Fingers" Louie," the full-time snitch and part-time safe cracker who had fled conviction and the city for Los Angeles, only to meet a worse ending, as DeWitt, who was there in the City of Angels, knew.

But some veteran guzzlers remained. DeWitt waved to "Two Fingers" Tony Mangiamangia, who had served as an excellent carver at Guido's Kosher Deli until he lopped off a pair of digits on his slicing hand. And there was poor "Southpaw Sammy" Stickitt yelling for him to come over and join him and his friends. Sammy probably had friends, but not at the Elbow, where now and customarily he sat drinking alone. Sammy's trouble was that he couldn't stop regaling the bar's patrons with sad stories of how he had been unrightfully banned from baseball. Gus told people that Sammy had given new meaning to the saying, "crying in one's beer."

DeWitt waved back to Sammy but kept his distance. He also was determined, for other reasons, to keep his distance from "Gardenia Gertie," who was staggering his way.

"Well how the hell is my favorite private dick? I haven't seen you for at least a week. Where have you been keeping yourself, and more to the point, wouldn't you like to keep yourself with me?" Gertie leered at him, her bright red lipstick painted on her mouth as if by a blind person. "We could go back to your place. I've never seen it, you know. We could go back to my place, of course, but come to think of it, I don't know if those two gents have put on their clothes and left yet."

"Another time, Gertie. I'm working on a case," he lied. Truth was he hadn't been working on a case for some time, but he was in enough trouble already without taking a chance on more at the hands of Gardenia Gertie, more commonly known to the male frequenters of The Elbow as "Gonorrhea Gertie."

As he was leaving, Dick heard Southpaw Sammy telling no one in particular that he could have gone to the major leagues if it hadn't been for that lousy baseball commissioner. Gus followed by asking DeWitt when he was going to pay his tab. Sad and sour notes to leave on.

DeWitt rose early the next morning, fixed breakfast, and mulled over going to church. Soldiers were praying in foxholes, he figured, and maybe he should offer up a few of his own supplications in hope that he would never find himself in a foxhole or anywhere near a war zone. The Man upstairs might listen to him, but then He might think that he was in church only to cadge a favor. What to do, what to do?

What I need, the gumshoe told himself, were laughs, and what better place to find them than in the movies? Dick went to the dilapidated garbage can in his dilapidated kitchen and pulled out an oil-soaked, five-day-old newspaper that he had used for wrapping spoilt sardines. He was in luck: the movie section remained in readable condition, though barely. He was in more luck when he saw that a midtown movie house was featuring "Ghosts on the Loose," with the East Side Kids. The film would provide a special treat, he figured, since various people had told him that he reminded them of Huntz Hall, one of the Kids. (Others had likened him to Stan Laurel.)

DeWitt grabbed his aged green fedora, walked uptown, plunked down his quarter at the ticket booth, bought some crunchy candy, grabbed a seat in the middle of the half-filled theater, and settled down for some needed diversion. He could have, and would have, had he had a choice, dispensed with the Pathé news that preceded the featured attraction. Graphic depictions of the war in the Pacific depressed him in thinking that one day, and a not too distant one at that, his kisser might appear in such footage. The news ended and "Action in the North Atlantic" lit up the screen. "Action in the North Atlantic"? Someone's made a big mistake, he thought. Tripping over a couple sitting on the aisle seats and spilling their popcorn, he caught up with an usherette and demanded an explanation. The latter asked him when was the last time he read the newspaper, because features in their theater changed every Friday. DeWitt was angry. Then he became angrier when the manager refused to refund his ticket. "I'll never come to your flea-ridden dump you call a movie house again," he promised. The manager retorted that he, DeWitt, should be out there doing something for his country instead of relaxing in a movie house.

The episode further depressed the gumshoe, as did the inordinate amount of booze that he swigged down during the remainder of the day.

Monday couldn't come soon enough for Dick, despite a hangover that felt larger than all the exhibits combined in the New York World's Fair of 1939. Polish Phil, he reckoned, would have returned home by early evening at the latest, so promptly at six he removed the ice bag from his forehead and made the call.

"Yeah?"

"Hi, Phil, it's your old buddy, Dick DeWitt. How's the trip?"

"Hey, Dickie, long time no see. Trip wasn't bad. What's up with you? How did you make out with the draft board?"

DeWitt explained the situation and asked his friend what he would do if faced with this dilemma. He could hear the retired cop breathing deeply and wondered what was running through his mind.

"You know, Dickie, if I were you—and I give thanks on bended knees that I'm not—I'd probably run for the hills. Let's face it: you don't have much of a life now, but at least you got a life, which you might not have if you see any action. Yeah, I'd say get a new identity and get your ass as far away as you can. But—and maybe I shouldn't say this but I'm going to—I had a nice talk with my cousin Louise, the one who's serving time on a manslaughter rap for having knocked off her abusive bastard husband and the one you've had the hots for even before then. Well, I gave Louise the long and short of your situation, and she said that she liked you a lot and hoped to see you when she gets out of the slammer, but that she could never have anything to do with a draft dodger. Was I wrong to tell you this?"

"No, Phil, you weren't wrong. You just made everything crystal clear: I am a dead man either way."

Chapter 2

DeWitt figured that basic training would not be as pleasant as a night on the town with Rita Hayworth or even Zasu Pitts. But in his worst nightmares he could not have conceived the misery it would inflict upon him.

It began when he had trouble getting off the bus that had brought him and other recruits to the training base in New Jersey. His suitcase, stuffed with several bottles of booze in addition to lesser necessities, seemed too heavy for his rarely exercised one-hundred-and-sixty-pound frame. He trudged along, falling behind the other recruits from the bus.

"Hey, Grandpa, you need some help?" barked a soldier, arms akimbo and with a look that would install fear in all but the most intrepid or foolish.

"Sure could, buddy. If you'll just carry this until I catch my breath, I'd be much obliged."

The soldier, his three stripes promising little assistance, snarled, "Get your hairy ass and fucking suitcase into the processing center pronto. And if you need some help, I'll be mighty pleased to kick that ass and shove your grip where no sun shines. Now get moving, mister!"

By the time DeWitt received a couple of painful shots in his arm and rear end, caught his fatigues and bed clothing as they were tossed at him, made his bed, and ate a meal that was edible but over too soon, he retired to bed, exhausted and unhappy. He thought of swigging a few gulps from his precious cache of liquids, but decided otherwise, not knowing if the Army had any prohibitions for inductees.

The next morning was still night as far as he was concerned. "Get your asses out of bed, hit the john, get cleaned and dressed, make your comfy beds, haul your sorry selves over to the mess hall, and then get back here on the double. Then," Sergeant Growell paused, "then we're going to have ourselves some fun."

DeWitt looked at the clock. The last time he had got up this early had been when he left Kathleen Laughlin's bed and apartment before her husband returned from his night job on the waterfront. He and his roughly forty recruit roommates did what the sergeant had ordered. Very few seemed pleased with their experience thus far. One of their number asked DeWitt, who was seemingly older than all the other trainees, how they caught him. "By surprise, fellow, by surprise."

Bed check time. Growell strolled down the aisles, chewing out those who had failed to make up their beds to his satisfaction and only a tad less so to those who had. DeWitt presented a special case. "Do you call this a neatly made up bed, mister?" he queried a man who had made up very few beds in his life. "Now you see this her quarter? When I toss it in the air and it comes down and hits the blanket, there should be no bounce. That is, if you've done it properly."

The sergeant and peacetime gumshoe looked at the quarter. "Thanks, Serge, I appreciate your advice and also the quarter. With my business being kind of slow these days, I can use all the help that's coming my way."

While the other recruits laughed or stifled their laughs, the sergeant told the gumshoe to give him ten. DeWitt told him that he did not have a dime on him but would find one. This was before his lights went out, compliments of a solid right to the side of his head from an unamused noncommissioned officer of the United States Army.

And this was just the beginning of recruit Dick DeWitt's problems. The long daily marches and runs blistered his feet, the heavy load that he toted on these outings pained his sagging back and shoulders. Before the war he had rarely carried anything heavier than hootch and hangovers. The day on the firing range in which he tripped and nearly shot the rifle instructor found him in much deeper trouble. Only Sergeant Growell's intervention saved him from a stay in the stir. It was not that the NCO had become soft on DeWitt. He merely wanted him nearby for more punishing chores. DeWitt's morale reached its low point when the sergeant forced him to clean the latrine with a pocket-sized toothbrush. And when the demoralized former private detective finished, the sadistic maker of mollusks into men forced him to do it again. This seemed all the harder for one who didn't make it a strict habit of brushing his set of thirty-twos daily in peacetime.

By the end of his second week on the base DeWitt was ready to call it quits. Looking back on his phone call with Polish Phil, he realized that he had made the wrong choice: if he served Uncle Sam he might one day win Louise's heart, but only maybe; on the other hand, if he had taken the Polack's advice and skipped town, he would now be happier and ultimately safer. Could have, should have, didn't.

Then one day when the recruits had returned to their barracks after a particularly grueling march, Sergeant Growell stuck his pocked face into the door. "Any of you cunts seen the army's biggest jerk?" Several heads swiveled toward DeWitt. "Oh yeah," Growell said, "I see America's number one threat to winning this war. Haul ass over here, Mr. Dimwit, I got a message for you."

DeWitt had no idea what his tormentor had in store for him but decided that it was more trouble.

"For some reason, General Shrapnell wants your company, probably for a nice cup of tea and some crumpets. So get the hell over to headquarters immediately. And if you miss chow," he smiled "there's always tomorrow."

Headquarters was a ten-minute walk away, but DeWitt, sore feet and all, hightailed it. Punctuality availed nothing in this case, and he was forced to wait half an hour before an aide said that the general would see him.

"At ease," the base commander ordered. "Well, soldier, reports on you show that you leave a lot—no, make that more than a lot—to be desired." He lit a Lucky Strike. "Nevertheless," he took a long drag, "nevertheless, someone for some damn fool reason wants you to undertake vital work for the country. Tell me, how are you related to Lieutenant General John L. DeWitt, the head of the Army's Western Defense Command?"

"I'm sorry, sir, but I don't know if I'm related to a General DeWitt." He looked thoughtful. "I did have a great uncle Jasper who was given the heave-ho from the Army for having attempted to desert, but a 'John L. DeWitt' I've never heard of. I have heard of a General Nuisance, of course."

General Shrapnell frowned. "Listen, soldier, get smart with me and you'll rot in the brig despite this call for your assistance. It must be a snafu. Some feeble-minded clerk saw your name and passed it on to Western Command. I doubt if Lieutenant General John L. DeWitt, busy as he is, has any knowledge of the matter. Someone made an assumption that proved incorrect. But I see here that you were a private detective before Pearl Harbor. Maybe that had something to do with it. I don't know and, frankly, at this point I don't care. It's my responsibility to see that our boys are fully prepared to fight, and that's that."

The general sifted through a few papers on his cluttered desk before he found DeWitt's orders. "According to this, soldier, you'll go by train the day after tomorrow to Los Angeles and report to… well, you can read it for yourself."

DeWitt could barely contain himself. "Yes, sir, I'm pleased to do anything to help my country in this time of need." He saluted. Before wheeling around to leave, he asked if he should know more about General DeWitt.

Don't you read the papers, private?" General DeWitt is in charge of relocating Japanese from the West Coast, where they could be acting as a fifth column to help their brethren in their war against us. He testified before congress that 'a Jap's a Jap' whether he or she was born here or in that heathen land across the Pacific. I remember his words that 'we must worry about the Japanese until he is wiped off the map.' A lot of people in California hated the Japs long before the war, but hate and fear shot up after the attack on Pearl. All the state's big shot politicians sided with General DeWitt, especially after an enemy submarine fired shells into Santa Barbara earlier this year, followed by a panicked response to a false report of Jap planes flying over Los Angeles. Shortly after Pearl, the U.S. government rounded up and held a number of noncitizen Japanese (Issei). Then in February the war department received a presidential order to remove any suspicious Issei from our military areas. Finally, the president ordered the relocation of the Issei, their American-born offspring (Nisei), and alien Japanese from the West Coast to further inland. It's estimated that by summer it will be a done deal: more than 400,000 of them will be living in camps fenced in with barbed wire and guarded by soldiers.

"My guess, soldier, is that this relocation relates to what you'll be doing. Now one more thing that I nearly forgot: your orders are marked 'top secret.' Do I need to remind you to keep this secret at all costs? And soldier, good luck."

After dismissing DeWitt, Shrapnell looked worried. "I hope I'm not making a mistake, Sam," he said to his aide. "I need to get on the good side of the higher ups—and that might include General John A. DeWitt– if I'm going to get a second general's star before I retire. I know that the vast majority of Japanese and Japanese Americans on the West Coast are good, loyal Americans, and that this Lieutenant General DeWitt has a bug up his ass about them. But I'm sending this idiot Dick DeWitt, who may be a relative, to his area of the war because it might be my last chance for promotion. On the other hand, I have a hunch that we'd win this goddamn war a hell of a lot sooner if Private DeWitt were fighting on the other side."

DeWitt—the private dick, that is—left the base commander's office whistling a Cole Porter tune and doing some dance steps that would have left Fred Astaire without envy. Am I glad to give up New Jersey and that fucking Sergeant Growell for sunny California? You bet!

On the appointed day and time, orders in hand, Private Dick DeWitt was en route to the City of Angels, but not before bidding farewell to Sergeant Growell and giving the startled NCO a big hug followed by a middle finger salute.

Chapter 3

Union Station. DeWitt's cross-country trip had been without significant incidents, and now, in early April 1942, he was back in the land of sun and sometimes fun. Those months he had spent in Los Angeles a few years ago had promised opportunities for a gumshoe whose business in New York had since become drier than the Sahara. Hollywood, especially, had provided allures, though the murder case he had become involved with didn't count as one of them. Now, no longer a civilian, he was here to fulfill his duty, whatever that would entail.

The Checker Cab DeWitt hailed outside Union Station took him to his new abode, as per orders, a small bungalow located on Miramar in downtown Los Angeles. It was not near Union Station, and the fare was not cheap. DeWitt considered giving the cabbie a tip and then thought better of it. "I'd give you something more than the fare, but I'm a G.I. and there's a war on," he explained. Unmoved, the cabbie told him to have a fine time fighting the Japs and don't hurry back. In fact, he needn't come back at all.

The bungalow pleased DeWitt, its decent sized living room, bedroom, and adequate kitchen, all freshly painted, presented an unexpected contrast to the small, messy apartment he called home back east and gave promise that his stint in the Army might provide an upside. Tossing his suitcase on the bed, he searched the ice box and shelves for food and drink. No luck. From the cab he had noticed a small grocery store two blocks away that now became his destination. A half hour later he returned to the bungalow, laden with some food and a lot of booze. Too tired from the train trip and the emotional wear and tear of his call to duty, he fixed himself a good helping of Jack Daniel's and a light but favorite meal consisting of two sandwiches that blended sardines with peanut butter and a dish of vanilla ice cream topped by a dill pickle. Afterwards he treated himself to more booze and a perusal of a daily newspaper that he had picked up along the way to the grocery store. The war news remained grim, but not for long: Dick DeWitt was ready to do his job and help save the nation.

After a good night's sleep the gumshoe was ready to report for duty. Not wishing to spring for another cab fare, he asked at the newsstand for directions. A friendly proprietor shook his head and told him that bus service was limited in the city, but there was one fairly nearby that would drop him off near City Hall and the Hall of Justice, both of which were near Union Station. Dewitt waited a half hour for the bus, stubbornly refusing to hail a cab to ensure that he would arrive at his destination at the appointed hour.

Nearly forty-five minutes late, an annoyed DeWitt found the building that quartered the branch of Army Intelligence. Bounding up the stairs to the third floor, he threw open the door and started yelling about the city's lousy bus service and how public transportation was so much better in the city he called home.

"Is that a fact?" asked an armed guard. "Well, we'll see if we can make you feel better, private. But first I think you should get your sorry ass in to see the colonel. He's been waiting for you for some time now, but I'm sure he'll be glad to write a letter of complaint to the city's bus line right away. He doesn't have much else to do."

The guard knocked on a closed door. "Yes, what is it?" a gruff voice demanded.

"It's that Private DeWitt to see you, sir."

"Send him in."

DeWitt walked in and gave the colonel a half-hearted salute. "That guard said you'd be glad to write a letter to the bus company to complain about their lousy service. Otherwise, I wouldn't have been late this morning, or at least not more than ten or fifteen minutes late."

Colonel Ezekiel Worthy peered over his glasses. "Is that so, private? Well, I'm so sorry that the nasty bus company inconvenienced you. I hope that you're not too upset." The colonel gnawed at his lower lip. "A few words, if I may, soldier, before I write that letter. First of all, if you ever have the colossal gall to show up late again for any reason whatsoever, I'll hang you by your hairy balls and then send you to Fort Leavenworth to spend the rest of your miserable life in solitary confinement. Is that clear? Secondly, if you ever come in here and offer that pitiful excuse for a salute, I'll make sure you'll never be able to raise your hand above your dick. What the hell did they teach you in basic training?

DeWitt looked confused. "But what about that letter to the bus company? Don't you think they deserve to hear about their poor service?"

Serving in Army Intelligence, the colonel encountered some bright soldiers, some considerably so. Was the man who stood before him a random variation, he wondered, slightly mad, or outright perverse. He wasn't sure.

"Private DeWitt, I'm going to forgive, or at least try to forgive, what's just been happening. We're at war now, and we need all the help we can get, even if it's not exactly the kind of help we would prefer. So sit down and I'll inform you of your duties. But first let me ask you what you know about spying. My guess is that you must know a good deal or the higher-ups wouldn't have sent you to me."

"Well, colonel, I don't like to blow my own horn, if you know what I mean, but I do know quite a lot about spying and spies. For instance," DeWitt smirked, "I read a lot about that Mata Hairy who spied for the Krauts during the last war and then took a bullet or two from the Limeys. He was a real good spy up to them."

The colonel's arched his eyebrows. "Don't you mean Mata Hari, who was a she and not a he?"

"Well, sir, maybe I read the wrong books or maybe I just forgot. It was a long time ago."

The colonel sighed. "Go on, private. Tell me what else you've learned about spies."

DeWitt thought for a while. "Aren't they a kind of apple? Sure they are. You mean to say that you never tasted one of those Northern Spies? Personally, I prefer McIntosh or Golden Delicious but frankly, apples were never my favorite fruit. I'll take bananas or pears or watermelons or..."

"That's enough, soldier. I don't have all day for this horseshit. Now let me tell you what you'll be doing while you're here." The colonel shuffled through a sheaf of papers. "I can put it in a nutshell. You'll be looking for enemy subversives, which is to say, anyone giving aid and comfort to the Japs. You might also sniff out some unfriendly Krauts and Wops, but the slant eyes are the main concern here on the Coast."

"You've got the right man for the job, sir. Back east I was an expert at sniffing out anything from big-time criminals to ladies' underwear."

The colonel stared at the gumshoe. "I don't care what the hell you were sniffing, soldier. Here you're going to do your job and duty as we see fit. You'll report here in person anytime you think there's a rat crawling around."

"How large a rat, sir? I mean where I came from there were rats as big as dogs. Shouldn't I call a pest control center rather than bother you?"

Swiveling in his chair to look out the window and cursing audibly, the man in charge took a few minutes before returning to the puzzled look on DeWitt's face.

"Soldier, they say that some people are not as dumb as they look. In your case, I'd say that you're much dumber than you look. If you don't learn the ropes—and quickly—I'm going to send you to say 'hello' to our Nip friends in the Pacific. Or I could change my mind and send you to Fort Leavenworth for the war's duration. My guess is that you'd be fit for cleaning latrines, especially with all the shit you're giving me. NOW BUCKLE UP!"

DeWitt looked down at his belt but saw no problem. Why is the colonel busting my balls? he wondered.

Sir, you've got nothing to worry about. Back in New York, people used to say, 'If the case can't possibly be solved, DeWitt's your man."

"I believe that, soldier. Now before I set you loose on the city, I "have a few more instructions. First, you'll always wear civvies, so that you won't stand out in the crowd as military. Second, you'll be discreet in your intercourse with others. And by that, I don't mean you'll use a condom whenever a piece of tail passes by. I mean don't blab. Spies and Axis sympathizers are everywhere, despite the internment camps. "As for funds, besides your regular army pay, you'll have an expense account, which is not, repeat not, for taking your ass to nightclubs like the Cocoanut Grove in the Ambassador Hotel or the Bowl in the Biltmore, or for picking up cuties who are more interested in picking you up, if you get my meaning. Now any questions? Good. And don't forget to pick up the address of your new quarters from the sergeant outside my office. You'll like the family you'll be staying with. They're one hundred percent patriotic, and the son will watch your back. You will be needing that, believe me. Good luck then. Dismissed!"

DeWitt felt like telling the colonel that he was capable of washing his own back, but the latter was already leafing through his sheaf of papers.

Chapter 4

DeWitt's relocated quarters lay in the heart of Chinatown on Broadway, only a few blocks distant from Union Station. Houses that interspersed neighborhood shops, both draped with signs he could not understand, the crowds jostling and speaking a language he could not fathom, and strange, sometimes hostile looks he received when he and his luggage exited the cab announced that he had arrived in a new world. "I'm here to win the war for my country," he said to himself as he took a deep breath of the city's mid-afternoon spring air mixed with the odors of Cantonese-style Chinese cooking. This was true—to an extent. Patriot though he assured himself that he was, he would have favored civilian life and its occasional private eye jobs, evenings at The Slippery Elbow with its colorful collection of lushes and semi-lushes, and an occasional night in the boudoir of some good-looking, preferably single dame.

The house, situated on Broadway, was a two-story wooden-frame structure that had seen its better days, better years, better decades. It hinted vaguely that pink or rose had been its original color, but only a desperate gambler would place a bet. Surprisingly, perhaps illogically, a well-tended lawn, complete with flowers and Buddha statuary, fronted the house, adding a touch of grace to its depressing exterior. DeWitt leaned on the buzzer a few times before the front door opened. "Whatcha want? We don't need no life insurance. My husband, he already dead."

Priding himself on his clever mind and vast experience as a gumshoe, DeWitt immediately guessed that the woman was none other than his hostess and landlady, Mrs. Lotus Blossom Chow.

"You must be Mrs. Chow. I'm Dick DeWitt, the new boarder Uncle Sam sent over."

The woman, short, plump, and with piercing eyes, asked "Why you not say so in first place?"

"I just did, Mrs. Chow."

"Okay, soldier boy, come in and I show you your room on second floor. My son, daughter, and me, we live on first floor with our five cats. My husband, poor man, he died when a streetcar run over him. I told him he drank too much, but he never listens to his little Lotus Blossom… that's me, Lotus Blossom Chow."

As she spoke, the soldier boy noticed a shy female standing in the hallway several feet behind them. She must have been in her late twenties, he guessed, but he knew how hard it was to figure out the age of colored people, whether they were yellow, black, whatever.

Sensing her presence, Lotus Blossom called her daughter to come and meet their new boarder. "Soldier boy, I like you to meet my only daughter, Feng Shui Chow. She good girl studying shorthand at some school. You will like talk to her. She very smart. Like her mother." She smiled. "Also, Mr. Soldier Boy, make sure you only talk with her. If you put hands on her, you will lose your… well, you know what you will lose. By the way, my son, who is at work now, is policeman here in Chinatown. He one tough guy."

"Feng Shui, make tea and put out nice almond cookies for this gentleman while I show him to room"

The room Mrs. Chow had set aside for her boarder was moderate sized and swept clean, though it smelled strongly of disinfectants. A single bed, an old table and chair, an older couch, and a badly scratched wardrobe made up its contents. The walls contained a few Chinese prints and scrolls. More eye-catching was the large American flag pasted above the bed's headboard. Unfortunately, it was upside down. A floor lamp and small desk lamp were meant to provide the room's artificial lighting; a view of the family garden in the substantial backyard promised decent daylight illumination.

"You like room, yes? Man who live here before you say it was good enough for Forbidden City in Peking."

"Why did he leave then?"

"Oh, he got killed in fight in opium den down the street. You like opium? I can get you good stuff," she whispered, "but don't say word to daughter Feng Shui or to policeman son. Okay?"

DeWitt nodded his assent and wondered what kind of situation he might be getting into.

"Let's go, soldier boy, and we have tea and almond cookies. Then we have good supper when son come home."

Unbeckoned company arrived as DeWitt was trying to figure where to put his civilian and military clothes, utility kit, and bottle of booze. The company announced itself with a variety of meows, purrs, and hisses. As DeWitt later ascertained from Mrs. Chow, the felines were Sing-li, Ting-li, Ming-li, Ling-li, and Chang-kai-Shek—four females and a menacingly large tom. Two of the furry quintet, including a snarling Chang, had situated themselves in his suitcase and showed no indication of vacating the premise. Letting discretion form the better part of valor, DeWitt decided to unpack after the tea and cookies.

The tea hit the proverbial spot, the cookies reminded him that, in the fast-paced events of the day, he had missed lunch. Mrs. Chow insisted that he have more tea and more of the almond cookies; Feng Shui insisted on remaining standing behind her mother and staring at DeWitt. "How come you have such big round eyes?" she asked.

An old nursery line came to mind: "The better to see you with, my dear." Feng Shui giggled and lowered her glance. Lotus Blossom neither giggled nor lowered her glance. "What you mean by that, soldier boy? You making round eyes at my daughter? Have I not warned you?"

DeWitt made amends as best he could. He did not intend to make Feng Shui blush, he protested, wondering even as he spoke if people with yellow skin could blush. "Everyone I know," he lied miles beyond the boundaries of little white lies, "will vouch that I am, and always have been, a gentleman."

The self-advertisement seemingly mollified Lotus Blossom, and the two continued to sip tea, consume cookies, and talk about this and that. Lotus was in high spirits until DeWitt brought up the subject of the war. The smile left her face and she began pounding on the table. "I hate those Japanese bastards. You know what horrible things they do to men, women, and children in Nanking? You know how they show no mercy?" She stopped to wipe her tears and paused to compose herself. "You know what I wish, soldier boy? I wish America build a big bomb, bigger than any one has even thought of, and then throw it down on all Japan. Yes, that is what I wish."

Conversation lagged; tea and cookies lay untouched. Feng Shui announced that she was going to her room to rest. A key opening the front door lock broke the painful lull.

"Hi, Ma, I'm home." The uniformed man who entered was Low Fat Chow, Lotus Blossom's be loved son and, though she would never admit to it, favorite offspring. He was tall and on the slim side. His handshake, made after introductions, proclaimed his strength, but the long raw scar that disfigured the left side of his face from ear to jawbone warned that pure strength does not necessarily triumph.

Low Fat was ravenous after a hard day on a hard job. He asked DeWitt to join him for some Tsingtao beer. DeWitt was happy to oblige, though he would have been happier to have a drink of hard stuff. While Lotus Blossom and Feng Shui prepared supper and set the table, the two men got acquainted and forged an early camaraderie. DeWitt, who was normally suspicious of anyone whose complexion was darker than his own, was surprised by Low Fat's likeability.

In addition to the requisite large bowl of rice, the evening meal consisted of a larger bowl that contained a serpentine figure in a kind of oily broth. "What is it?" DeWitt asked. Lotus Blossom beamed and said that it was a special dish she made for special guests. "It is fresh, Mr. DeWitt."

DeWitt, who feared slithery reptiles almost as much as he had feared his former wife, controlled incipient nausea. "Did I see its head move?"

"Oh yes," Lotus Blossom answered. "Daughter Feng Shui insist that eel is best when still living. But do not worry. It will not bite you once you eat it." Mother and daughter burst into raucous laughter; Low Fat looked embarrassed; DeWitt asked where the bathroom was.

After retching, DeWitt returned to find the Chow family heatedly speaking in Chinese. "We sorry you no like my cooking, Mr. DeWitt. Everyone else likes eating eel, especially when it's still alive."

DeWitt somehow managed not to race back to the bathroom. Forcing a weak smile, he tried to squirm out of the embarrassing predicament. "Sorry, Mrs. Chow, it must have been something I ate for lunch. I think I'll take a walk now. A little fresh air might do the trick."

"Only a goddamn Chink would serve an eel, and a living one at that," the soldier boy swore to himself. "What's for the next meal? One of their cats?"

DeWitt strolled to nearby Union Station and found a diner. With nearly all the counter stools and booths occupied, decided that the food would be more to his liking than that served up by Lotus Blossom Chow. His guess proved correct. The liver and onions, which he laced with a generous helping of mayonnaise and a dash of tabasco sauce, did the trick. He walked out of the diner a contented man. Whether he heard the waitress yelling that he had not left a tip remains a mystery.

While walking back to his dwelling on Broadway, he pondered his first move in keeping his country free from enemies. According to the package of instructions that accompanied the Chows' address handed to him that morning, he was to reconnoiter Little Tokyo. DeWitt knew shit from Shinola better that what was meant by reconnoiter, but rather than call headquarters, he decided to explore the nearby area in the morning.

When he returned to where he was staying, he found Lotus Blossom and Feng Shui deeply engaged in playing some sort of game, and Low Fat improving his education via *The Police Gazette*. DeWitt said good night; the women said nothing; the son grunted.

Once upstairs, Dick remembered that he had not fully unpacked his possessions. Striding over to the open suitcase, he noticed a foul, sour smell and a good deal of wetness inside the luggage. His years as a gumshoe once again put him on the scent, so to speak: the $‸#@%‸& cats had peed all over the contents.

Chapter 5

DeWitt was in a foul mood when he awoke after a restless night of tossing and turning on an uncomfortable mattress and finding the stench of feline urine continuing to odorize the items in his suitcase.

"Mrs. Chow, did you know that your cats peed in my suitcase while I was not in my room yesterday?"

"Why they do that?

"How should I know? They're your damn cats," he sputtered.

"You think I tell them to go pee-pee?" soldier boy. "You think Lotus Blossom do such thing even to round eye?

DeWitt managed to contain his rage, not least of all because of the meat cleaver his landlady was holding. The two then brokered an uneasy truce. The soldier promised not to harm any of the cats; the landlady promised not to let her pets into his room. As a bonus, Lotus Blossom threw in the location of a nearby laundry where he could take his soiled clothing.

After gathering his dirty items into an old, ragged pillowcase Lotus Blossom had given him, he took out and wiped the urine-coated bottle of Jack Daniel's from his suitcase and took a few swigs. Then he took another and decided to hunt down subversives. After all, he told himself, I am a law-abiding, one hundred percent American patriot.

A man need not express his love of country on an empty stomach, DeWitt told himself, as he headed for the diner that fed him last evening's meal. On the way he stopped off at the recommended laundry. The wizened man behind the counter smelled what DeWitt handed him and asked if he often wet himself. DeWitt refrained from telling the geezer off or from what he preferred to do, namely, give his yellow skin a deeply purplish hue. He again kept his anger in check, not because he respected the man's race or age, but because he feared the man might have a weapon under the counter or have connections with the feared criminal Tongs who terrorized Chinatown.

The block before the diner featured a smoke shop that sold newspapers, all of them in Chinese. The proprietor professed not to know where DeWitt could find English-language ones, but the look on his face, like that on the laundry man's, bespoke an aversion to outsiders, as did his mutterings as DeWitt left.

The sign on the diner, in contrast, promised a friendlier welcome: "Chinese-American Food. All Welcome." The morning rush hour—if indeed there had been a rush hour—had peaked, leaving behind a few stray patrons, a man behind the counter, a cook, and a cashier sitting on a high stool next to the door. The lone waitress tottered to his table as though her feet had been bound, tradition-style in old China, as a child. She flung down a menu. "Likee bleakfast special?" she asked. "It good and plenty, just like the candy." She smiled, exposing an occasional tooth.

DeWitt, unable to decide if he wanted Chinese or American food, ordered both. "Gimme some of your mooshu pork with a side order of bacon and sausages. Yeah, and I'll have a root beer to wash it down with."

The waitress nodded and moved unsteadily away, saying something that sounded like "Clazy Amelican."

While waiting for his breakfast to arrive, DeWitt walked up to the cashier in hope that the latter could suggest where an English-language newspaper might be found.

"You bet I know where you can find a newspaper you can read. Right here." The cashier reached down and pulled up the morning edition of the *Los Angeles Times.* You want to read about the war, yes? We're going to kick the you know what out of those Japanese bastards or my name isn't Sammy Burpp."

DeWitt stared at the cashier. He doesn't look like a Sammy Burpp, he thought, but he doesn't look like an egg foo yung, either.

"Yeah, we're going to win this war, all right. By the way, if you don't mind my asking, are you yellow or white?"

The smile faded from Sammy Burpp's face. "I'm both. My mother was Cantonese and my father was a round eye like you. He was a merchant sailor who met my mother after he was shanghaied in San Francisco and taken to Shanghai. A couple of years later they came to Los Angeles and here I am," he laughed.

"But what are you doing here? I saw you last evening. I know my food is good, but why are you here again so soon, if I may ask?"

DeWitt had to think on his feet, although he would have preferred thinking while comfortably seated. He didn't want to blow his cover, so he knew that he'd better come up with a believable story."

"My name is Dick DeWitt. I'm a rice salesman, and I know how you Chinamen and half-Chinamen love your rice. So here I am in Chinatown."

Burpp's eyebrows shot up. "Oh, and where does this rice come from?"

DeWitt thought fast. "Well, most of it comes from Indiana."

Burpp's eyebrows shot up skyrocketed.

"But not all of it. Some comes from New Jersey. Weehawken, I think."

The cashier stroked his chin. "Tell me, Mr. DeWitt, do you have time while you're here to sightsee? Chinatown has many delights, if you know what I mean, and..." He brought his face nearer. "Now that they've begun putting those accursed Japs into camps, Little Tokyo is not to be missed, especially by a sensitive man such as yourself. You are a sensitive man, are you not?"

"You bet I am. When I shave I nick myself and get a rash. That runs in the family. My great uncle Clinton DeWitt used to say that shaving was the work of the Devil. I guess that's why he refused to shave until the vermin in his beard began to itch too much."

"I see your point, Mr. DeWitt. Tell me, I know someone, a frequent visitor to my humble diner, who would enjoy giving you a first-class tour of Chinatown and Little Tokyo, which is. Would you be interested in availing yourself of her services? She's also very beautiful and speaks English perfectly"

Manna from heaven. DeWitt couldn't believe his good fortune. Now he could get the lay of the land and... no, he mustn't get too distracted. Uncle Sam was counting on him to help win the war.

He thanked the owner, who told him to return the next morning around 8:00 or 8:30 and his guide would be waiting. And enjoy today's breakfast, he added.

DeWitt did enjoy his repast, although he failed to take note of the grease that fell from the plate and stained his only clean pair of trousers. He nearly tipped the waitress but settled for paying the cashier and giving a hearty burp to Mr. Burpp. "See you tomorrow," he promised.

DeWitt could have begun exploring Little Tokyo on his own, but frankly he had no idea of what a Japanese spy, saboteur, or fifth columnist might look like, save that his skin was either light, medium, or dark yellow. Even so, he asked himself, how was he to distinguish a Chink from a Nip? They all look alike, don't they? No, he'd better wait for the next day and the knowledgeable assistance of the dame Burpp had recommended.

Self-satisfied, he spent the late morning in a nostalgic haze, exploring some of the sites he well remembered from several years ago when he had worked on the case of the Hollywood Starlet: the apartment he shared with Marty "Mumbles" Hardy on Bunker Hill; the spacious Brookdale Cafeteria, the world's largest; and the Pink Pussycat Lounge, where he first met the luscious starlet Scarlett. But he hadn't forgotten that Hollywood had nearly killed him. Now he only had to worry that anyone with yellow skin might finish the job. As the exasperated Oliver Hardy said to his friend, Stanley Laurel, "And here's another fine mess."

Chapter 6

Lack of sleep the previous night and the long walking tour of old haunts afforded DeWitt peaceful hours of slumber. Knowing that he had a rendezvous at Burpp's diner somewhere between 8:00 and 8:30, he left a note on the kitchen table for Lotus Blossom to knock on his bedroom door at 7:00, which she failed to do. Fortunately, the blood-curdling screams of Lotus and Feng Shui, and two other Chinese women, did the trick at 8:15. He threw on his clothes (the ones he had worn both yesterday and the day before, having forgotten to pick up the clean ones at the laundry) and thundered down the steps.

"Why you up so early, soldier boy?"

"What do you mean early? I left you a note to wake me at 7:00."

Lotus Blossom rolled the dice before looking up.

"No. You write "9:00," not 7:00. They no teach you how to write in school?"

DeWitt's instinct was to propel the Mah Jongg tiles onto the floor, pick up the board, and bash in Lotus Blossom's head. But the need to rush to the diner prevailed.

Dodging traffic and giving the bird to the owner of the smoke shop, he made it to the diner a little before 9:00. His basic training in New Jersey notwithstanding, he was out of breath. He had not raced this quickly since an angry husband had chased him with a blowtorch.

"I thought you had changed your mind," said a concerned-looking Sammy Burpp.

"No, my worthless landlady didn't rouse me."

"Sit down and have some breakfast. Your guide stepped out for a few minutes but promised she would soon return. She told me that you should wait for her and that she would make it worth your while."

DeWitt wasn't so sure that she would, but he knew he had to garner information for Colonel Worthy, and the sole piece of solid information he could now report was that Chinatown had a lot of Chinese. With only that, he feared he might be sent to a hotspot in the Pacific, where the most important bit of information was that a helluva lot of Nips wanted to kill a helluva lot of Americans.

The diner, like the previous day, was mostly empty. DeWitt sat at the same table as then and waited for the same waitress to make her painful way to him.

"You like same as yesterday?"

"No, I think I'll have something simple. How about some corn flakes, a side order of sardines, a glass of grapefruit juice, and a cup of java?"

"Solly, we no have java. Maybe you like coffee?"

"Yeah, great."

"Solly, but we have only tea this morning. Good tea."

"Skip it."

"I no can skip. I have bad feet."

DeWitt was undecided as to whether he should step on the waitress' foot or swat her on the head with her stack of menus. But just then the door opened for a newcomer, whom Burpp greeted with gusto.

"Here she is, Mr. DeWitt. I want you to meet your guide, Miss Rosie O'Grady."

DeWitt did a double take. The guide, who looked in her late twenties or early thirties, was slim and of medium height, with jet black straight hair that hung half way down her back. She was wearing a tight-fitting classy dress, its slit running well above her knees. The soldier boy concluded that she would have been a knockout if it weren't for her nose, which was too large for the rest of her face and sported a bump in the middle.

Then, too, her name belied her Asian features. "Are you 'Sweet Rosie O'Grady' or just sweet, or just Rosie O'Grady?" DeWitt asked, much pleased with himself for the witticism.

The woman darted a puzzled look at the diner's owner, who told her that "Sweet Rosie O'Grady" was an old-time song.

"Rosie, why don't you sit down with Mr. DeWitt and get acquainted before you set out on your sightseeing. Besides, he hasn't had his breakfast yet, and I'm sure he'll need it."

Rosie sashayed over to where DeWitt was sitting and announced that she was all his for the day.

"How about the night, too?"

The look on Rosie's face showed displeasure. "Is that a joke, Mr. DeWitt? I'm not that kind of woman," she retorted.

Dick usually didn't understand when he gave offense—which was much of the time—but he did on this occasion and apologized as best he could. "It was only a joke, sweetie. Everyone knows I'm a real gent."

"I forgive you." She smiled. Sort of. "Here comes Ping Pong with your breakfast. Enjoy it, and then we'll get started."

After plopping down DeWitt's breakfast, the waitress turned to Rosie: "Missy like cup of coffee?"

DeWitt began to choke on the spoonful of cereal and sardines he had shoved into his mouth. "Hey Ping Pong, or Bing Bang, or Ding Dong, or whatever your name is, you told me that you didn't have any coffee."

"We have no coffee then but I bring you some now. Okay?"

While devouring his meal, the gumshoe and his guide got better acquainted.

"Mr. Burpp told me that you are a rice salesman, Mr. DeWitt—or "Dick," as you say you prefer. How fascinating! How did you get into that line of work?"

"To tell the truth, Rosie," Dick said as he wiped a helping of corn flakes and sardines that had fallen onto his trousers, I love rice so much that I wanted to bring it into the lives and stomachs of my fellow humans. I've always been the kind, generous sort, so I followed my calling."

"That's wonderful, Dick. Your mother must have been so proud when you did."

"To be honest, Rosie, she was a little sore that I didn't become a proctologist. She said that the work and I made a perfect match. I'm not sure why, but then mom was a little hard to understand. But I just couldn't get over my dream of selling rice, if you know what I mean."

"But how about you, Rosie? You look like a Chink... er, a Chinaman... er, I mean a Chinese gal. But how'd you get your name?"

She darted a sharp look at DeWitt. "My father was an American soldier who went to rescue Westerners from the siege of Peking during the Boxer Rebellion at the end of the nineteenth century. There he met my mother, who was a servant to an English couple. Soldier and servant fall in love, make love, and some years later have daughter, who now is sitting in front of you. Sadly, both parents are dead, and I am alone."

DeWitt waited while she shed some tears and blew her prominent nose.

"But what do you do now to make ends meet?

Rosie smiled. "I do different things. I paint and sell my water colors, and I am a part-time hostess in a nightclub. That helps to pay the rent and keep me from being a concubine or a down-and-out woman of the streets."

"You got real guts, Rosie. Now if you don't mind my saying, you also got a real schnoz. Hell, it's almost as big as Jimmy Durante's. Where'd you get that from, your mother's side or your father's? I've never come across a Chin... a Chinese person with a beak that size, and a broken one to boot.

"Are you always this sensitive, Mr. DeWitt?"

"Well, thanks, Rosie. I think you're the first person who's called me sensitive. But I just say what's on my mind. I believe in calling a spade a spade and a Ch ... You know what I mean."

"Yes, I certainly do know what you mean. If you must know, I got my nose from jiu-jitsu."

"Who's this jiu guy? I know the Jews have their faults—plenty of them—but going around beating up women is not one of them. Anyway, I wish they'd go around and beat up all those Kraut Nazi bastards who are making their lives hell."

Rosie, though continuing to seethe inwardly, explained that jiu-jitsu was an ancient skilled Japanese martial art. "Believe me," she said, "I'd like to demonstrate it if we had more time."

"That's real white of you, but I guess you're right. We'd better get started on our tour. Shall we split the check or do you want to pay for your own?"

After paying their respective checks and saying good-by to the proprietor, they left the diner.

"While we're walking to Little Tokyo, Mr. DeWitt, I'm going to give you some background that might help you to peddle your rice and maybe, just maybe, enlarge your knowledge about people you know absolutely nothing about."

DeWitt was insulted. He knew there were Nips and Chinks, and that his country was at war with one of them. He also knew the color of their skins and the strange shape of their eyes, as well as the funny way they spoke. Hell, how much more did he need to know? he wondered.

Before the war, Rosie explained, a thriving Little Tokyo existed. During the 1920s it had been a hotbed for drugs and prostitution, but much less so since then. Most of the more than 30,000 Japanese Americans who lived in Los Angeles and Los Angeles County were decent, hardworking, law-abiding, and family-oriented. Restricted by law from owning land outright, they earned their living largely by growing fruits and vegetables on rented land or as fishermen. Anglos respected their agricultural prowess but continued to disrespect, if not downright despise, them for their race. This had been the lot of both Japanese and Chinese since they came to the United States in the latter nineteenth century. Their children—the Nisei, in the case of the Japanese, fared little better. And the more discrimination continued undiminished, the more those discriminated against remained a close-knit group, fearful, secretive, and, in turn, despising outsiders.

DeWitt asked Rosie why she had any sympathy whatever for yellow-bellied Japs. After Pearl Harbor, how could anyone say anything good about them.

"Mr. DeWitt," Rosie said in a low voice while looking about, "the Japanese have an ancient culture, much older than that of Americans, and that culture has produced much that is fine and beautiful. Japan has a long warrior history, it is true, but the attack on Pearl Harbor was not the work of all of its people. Do you understand?"

"Yeah. Well sort of."

Rosie could tell he wasn't convinced, but that wasn't her problem. Her problem was getting through the day with this coarse, vulgar idiot.

DeWitt, perceptive gumshoe that he was, noted a paucity of people on the streets and a plethora of small shops that posted "Closed" signs in English and signs in Japanese that he assumed relayed much the same message. He could tell from people entering and exiting both the Shinto temple on Jackson Street and the Buddhist one that stood near the intersection of First Street and Central Avenue that religious sites continued to offer comfort, but too few in number, at least on this day.

"Rosie, I'm hungry. All this walking around has worked up my appetite. Any chance for chowing down somewhere near?"

"As a matter of fact there is. The Black Samurai is only a few blocks from here. It's remained open ever since the government has started relocating Japanese. I've eaten there a few times myself and can vouch for the food. Maybe today they'll have the house specialty, broiled eel."

A few minutes later, having agreed to skip lunch, Dick DeWitt and Rosie O'Grady parted company, but not before exchanging phone numbers and promising to keep in touch.

Chapter 7

"Private DeWitt? This is Sergeant Grimm calling from Army Intelligence. The colonel wants you to haul your ass over here on the double. And between you and me, he's in a worse mood than usual."

"Can I have breakfast first?"

"DeWitt, haul your stinking ass over here NOW! Is that understood?"

It was understood. DeWitt arrived at Army Intelligence as soon as he finished breakfast.

"Come in."

"Good morning, colonel. Nice day, isn't it? Is Los Angeles always this nice this time of year?"

"Sit down and shut up, private. I called you here because I want an account of your activities and whether or not you've been putting our taxpayers' money to good use." The colonel lit up a cigarette. "Well?"

"Well, sir, I think that you'll agree that I've learned a lot so far. A couple of days ago a dame—half-Chink and half-Mick—showed me around Niptown. Weren't many of the yellow devils on the streets, but I got a pretty good idea of the lay of the land. And," DeWitt made a face, "I found out that they like to eat eel, just like the Chinks you've got me boarding with."

The colonel took a long drag on his cigarette, gave DeWitt a hard look, and asked what else he had learned.

The private looked puzzled. "Isn't that pretty good for a guy who's been on the job for less than a week? Believe me, colonel, you and our country have nothing to worry about. When Dick DeWitt puts his nose to the ground and gets a whiff of the scent, well... you've made a good bet that your horse is going to come in a winner. My motto as a private eye was 'If you need a dick, Dick's your man'."

The colonel swore to himself that if he and the Army needed a dickhead, they need look no further.

"Private, I want and need results, and pronto. I don't give a flying fuck about whether or not Japs like eel. I want to know if any of them still not in relocation centers are up to no good, and you're going to find this out for me, or you'll be vacationing in the South Pacific and saying 'hello' to a mess of Tojo's cruelest. Understood? Now get out before you make me angry."

"Ah, sir, you seem a little angry now."

"GET OUT!"

The colonel collected himself before asking Sergeant Grimm to bring him some water and a couple of aspirins. Grimm responded with alacrity. The colonel popped out a couple of analgesics from the bottle but refused the water. "I think I need something stronger than that." Reaching into the right-hand bottom drawer of his standardized military desk, he pulled out a half-empty bottle of Jim Beam, threw the headache-killers into his mouth, and tossed them down with the booze.

"I'm telling you, sergeant, every time I meet that goofball I'm thankful that I'm not carrying my sidearm. He may be the worst disaster this country has faced since the debacle at Pearl. I want to win this goddamn war, get a promotion, retire, and live out my years doing some fishing up in Oregon, where I have a small place that the missus and I just love. And, sergeant, I'm not going to let this chicken shit private eye from New York screw this up. No siree! And you know what we're going to do? We're going to take action. I can't get rid of the numbskull or my chances of promotion are about as good as his are for winning the Medal of Honor. But I can use some collateral help. Grimm, contact our gal G.I. and tell her that I wish to see her ASAP."

The sergeant suppressed a smile. He had contacted the attractive young woman before with orders to meet the colonel when he was working late.

Chapter 8

"We must be very, very careful. A gentle breeze does not always mean good weather."

"Yes, Ichiban. [number one]

"He is a sly, cunning foe."

"Yes, Ichiban."

"He wishes to undo all the plans we have for this accursed country."

"Yes, Ichiban."

"He calls himself Dick DeWitt."

"Yes, Ichiban. Do you wish me to kill him?

"Not yet. No, first we must find out if there are others who are assisting him in looking for those of us who remain loyal to our Land of the Rising Sun. We must not cut off the head of one snake if others continue to slither in the grass. We must cut off the heads of all such serpents. Do you understand?"

"Yes, Ichiban."

"Good. May our Emperor, the descendant of the goddess Amaterasu, guide us on our path."

Chapter 9

Brilliant ideas come to brilliant people, sometimes to lesser minds, and, occasionally, to the least expected minds. Unfortunately, the latter are also all too often choice receptacles for moronic ideas, such as the one that ensnared Pfc. Richard DeWitt.

Having failed to encounter enemy spies no matter how many times he walked up and down the mostly deserted streets of Little Tokyo—even after he had once asked a startled Japanese elderly lady if she knew of any spies or otherwise disloyal Japanese–he was at his wit's end. *If I report back to that mean sonofabitch colonel empty-handed, he may send me to fight in the Pacific. So what can I do?* he mused.

Then it hit him as he sat polishing off a plate of meat loaf smothered with sauerkraut and jalapeños in the Brookdale Cafeteria: those sly Nips may have caught on that he was a spycatcher. What he needed now was a disguise. "Why didn't I think of this before?" he shouted, as he banged his hand down, missing the table but not his meatloaf, and eliciting startled stares from nearby diners. He sprang from his seat and ran to the cashier, demanding to look at the phone directory's Yellow Pages. When the man informed him that it was not for public use, DeWitt shot back that he was a spycatcher working for the government, and that if the cashier didn't want to join our forces fighting the Nips, he'd better fork over the pages. Despite the pleas, angry shouts, and name-callings from a growing line of diners queuing to pay for their meals, DeWitt remained immovable, searching for… he wasn't sure. He slammed shut the Yellow Pages and left to strident jeers.

He returned to the Chow household, where he found mama and daughter Chow accusing one another of cheating at Mah Jongg, and son, Low Fat, listening to "The Green Hornet" on the Silvertone radio that graced the living room.

"Hello, Dick, why don't you sit down and listen to 'The Green Hornet'? It's almost over."

DeWitt liked the series, especially since it featured a master crime fighter like himself, but tonight he had something troubling his mind and couldn't concentrate on the Hornet's fictitious problems. Once the program finished and the commercials came on, he turned to Low Fat.

"Low Fat, I'm in a bind. You know what the Army wants me to do, but I'm getting nowhere. I'm determined to get somewhere, however, and what I need is a good disguise so that the Japs won't guess who I am or what I'm supposed to be doing. I could use suggestions, especially since you're a copper and might know a lot about the subject."

Low Fat lit up a Camel and frowned. Then he looked at DeWitt and smiled. "I'll tell you what, Dick. Why don't you go as a pachuco?"

"A what?"

"A pachuco. Haven't you guys from back east heard of them?

Well let me tell you something about them. They're Latinos, as you might guess by the name, more often than not teenagers or young men, and rebels. They don't like Anglos, and the feeling is fully reciprocated. So far there hasn't been any real trouble with them, but the police and the city's authorities are keeping an eye on them just in case. And it's plenty easy to keep an eye on them," Low Fat chuckled. "They like to wear what we call zoot suits, wide-lapelled long jackets coming to their knees, pegged trousers with a high waist, a big brimmed hat, and a watch dangling from a key chain. They're not hard to miss if you're looking in the right parts of the city."

"Where can I find this getup?"

The policeman laughed until he saw the serious expression on the spy-catcher's face.

"You're not kidding, are you pal?"

"Uh, uh."

"Listen, Dick, I've got some time tomorrow. I'll drive you to a costume shop I know, where you can pick from a wide variety of costumes. But sashaying around like a pachuco is certainly going to draw attention. Are you sure this is a wise move?"

"Yeah, Low Fat, it is. You see, nobody's going to take me for a spycatcher this way, but I can spy on them all I want without arousing suspicion. I'm cut out for this kind of work. Keep in mind, Low Fat, people couldn't get over what I did as a detective in New York."

"Okay. It's your decision. But I truly hope that it won't be your funeral.

Good as his word, Low Fat drove DeWitt to the costume shop the next day. He couldn't contain his laughter when he saw DeWitt garbed as a pachuco, complete with a cheap watch hanging from a corroded key chain. The pachuco wannabe, however, took a long look in the mirror and concluded that it was not bad. "In fact," he said to Low Fat, "I kind of like it. Everything suits me, except for the hat. Fortunately, I brought my green fedora to LA with me. I always wore it when I worked as a private eye."

DeWitt insisted on immediately wearing his new outfit rather than his regular street clothing when they left the store. He also suggested that they go to a bar—any bar—to check on the reaction he would get.

Low Fat said no, not for all the rice in China, and told DeWitt to get into the car.

Chapter 10

The following morning DeWitt put on his disguise and grabbed his green fedora and a pair of sunglasses. He went downstairs, kicking two of the cats aside. For the first time in any of the mornings since his arrival, Lotus Blossom, Feng Shui and the Chinese women with whom they were playing stopped arguing over their Mah Jongg game and looked at the soldier boy tenant. Only he did not look like any soldier they had ever seen.

"Hey, mister, you too early for Halloween. Army tell you to dress like that, or maybe you gone clazy." Lotus Blossom looked at her daughter for confirmation. "What you think, Feng Shui?"

I think he eat too much eel."

DeWitt managed a weak smile and left before his appetite for breakfast left him.

Sammy Burpp's Chinese-American diner promised a good way for DeWitt to find out if his disguise fooled others, as he was convinced it would.

"Hello, Dick, we've missed you," said the proprietor. Stifling a laugh, he asked if he was getting ready for Halloween.

DeWitt chose not to comment but to take his usual table and pay as little attention as possible to the increased volume of chatter from astonished patrons.

Ping Pong limped to the table with a menu. "Today not Halloween, Mister. You look like shit."

DeWitt scowled. "Do you know who I am?"

"You think I forget man who order foolish bleakfasts? Maybe that why you look like shit today."

DeWitt finished an order of toast and coffee and gave no thought of sur-
rendering a tip to Ping Pong. No likee my clothes, he told himself, go fuckee
yourself.

The gumshoe arrived back at the Chow house in a sour mood. Breakfast
had been a disappointment, more so his failure to have fooled anyone with his
disguise. I'm at sixes and sevens, he told himself, though he hadn't the faintest
idea of what the saying meant.

"Hey, soldier boy, you got woman waiting for you in living room. You make
date with hooker?" asked Mrs. Chow as soon as her boarder entered. "This is
good house I run. You not bring one of those women here, you understand?"

Mrs. Chow's outburst caught DeWitt off guard. "Listen, Lotus Blossom, I've
never gone with hookers," he lied. "With my good looks and charm, why would
I need to?"

Lotus Blossom stared at his outfit and told him not to keep the woman waiting and by no means take her up to his room."

"Hello, Dick. Remember me?"

"Yeah, I do Rosie. Have you been keeping your nose clean?"

"Yes, Dick, I have. How about you? How are they hanging—that is, if they're
still hanging?"

What a great kidder this dame is, he thought. I didn't know she had such a
subtle sense of humor.

"So what brings you here, Rosie?"

"I'm here to invite you to a party that some of my friends are throwing.
They're an interesting group, and I think you may enjoy meeting them, especially since you probably haven't made many acquaintances since you've been
here. And who knows," she said, "you might be able to sell them some rice. It's
this Saturday. I have a car and can pick you up around 8:30. Are you free?"

"Well, I've got a few other things lined up that night, but, sure, I think I can
arrange it. You want a drink or you got other irons to fry?"

Rosie told him she had to leave. On her way out she said good-bye to
Mrs. Chow, who growled something in Chinese before returning to the kitchen
table and her seemingly endless game of Mah Jongg with Fen Shui and their
two usual co-players

Dick, his stomach rumbling, decided to set off to the Brookdale Cafeteria for
an early lunch platter of spaghetti with a side order of rice and pickled herring,
the thought of which lifted his spirits.

Chapter 11

Came the evening of the party DeWitt wanted to impress both Rosie and the guests. Though not in the habit of bathing more than a few times monthly, he immersed himself in the Chow's semi-clean tub for a half hour of soaking and meditation. A quick shave and the selection of attire followed: more or less clean underwear, trousers, shirt, and a tie whose dark hues muted a miscellany of food stains. His white sox complimented his white sneakers. Not bad, he told himself looking into the mirror, not bad at all.

A car horn honked repeatedly outside the Chow home promptly at 8:30. DeWitt donned his green fedora, snapped its brim forward, and headed out for a night of diversion and—who knew?—possibly a lead or two in his quest for looming Nip spies.

Stepping into the dark Plymouth, he smelled the strong scent of perfume. "Hi, Rosie, what's that you're wearing, Channel 5?"

"Hi yourself, Dick. No, Chanel No. 5 is too rich for my pocketbook. Lilly Sachet suits me fine."

"It suits me fine, too, if you get my drift, and I'm sure getting the drift of your perfume," he said, ogling her.

"Well thank you. I can't tell what aftershave lotion you're wearing. Is it Bay Rum? Old Spice? What?

"Nah, it's just some cheap stuff I picked up in a Woolworth's. Anyway, not many dames have complained so far."

DeWitt asked Rosie how her work was going. "It's okay. I like being a hostess, even if where I work could use classier customers. But an unmarried gal like me will do almost any kind of work as long as it's legal. But tell me how the rice business is going."

"How should I... oh, it's a bit slow now, but I'm sure things will pick up. Rumor has it that there's a big Chink... er, Chinese wedding next week and... hey, tell me, do they throw rice like normal people do when the marrieds leave for their honeymoon? I suppose the rice is not cooked, right? I'll have to take that into consideration when I make my sales pitch."

"I can't help you there, Dick. I've never been to a Chinese wedding. You'll have to figure this out for yourself."

DeWitt was in a talkative mood, but Rosie cautioned that she had to pay attention to her driving. It was a dark night with no visible moon, and finding her way deep into the Hollywood Hills presented a problem on the clearest of nights.

The house was large, very large, with a circular gravel driveway highlighted by what DeWitt called a Port Cochise, although he confessed not knowing why anyone would call it after a bloodthirsty Apache. Rosie parked her car in the driveway and put her arm in DeWitt's as they passed under the porte-cochere to the front door. They rang the bell, which was answered by some sort of Asian servant—a Chink, a Filipino, maybe just a down-and-out actor from Central Casting who need an extra buck or two.

"Good evening," the servant said as he bowed. "May I take your hat, sir?"

"I'll keep it on, if you don't mind." DeWitt warily replied to the request for his green fedora from this total stranger.

"Ah, there you are!" The voice belonged to their host, who looked even more like an actor from Central Casting than the servant. He was tall, wore a tuxedo, and held a lit cigarette in a long, golden holder. The monocle he sported in his right eye augmented his elegant appearance, except when it slipped, which it did with some regularity. A medal attached to the lapel of the tuxedo provided the finishing touch.

Liebchen! You have not been here for such a long time, dearest Fräulein. You shouldn't disappoint an old man like me." He bowed and kissed Rosie's hand.

"My dear count, let me introduce you to my friend, Dick DeWitt. He's a rice salesman."

The count's monocle again slipped. "You are welcome to my party, Herr De-Witt. I am Count Ulrich Ditter von Puffendorff.

"From your name, count, I'm guessing that you're a Krau... German, and that the thing you got pinned on your penguin suit did not come from a Crackerjack box. Am I right?"

Rosie blushed and the count turned a deep shade of red but was able to regain his composure. "You are correct, Herr DeWitt. I left my homeland after that Herr Hitler took control. What you see on my tuxedo is an Iron Cross Third Class, a medal I won for my courage during the Great War. Now if you'll excuse me, I must see to my other guests. But please enjoy drinks and refreshment, and mingle with others." The count bowed and kissed Rosie's hand and gave DeWitt a look that no one could mistake for friendliness.

A couple of young female servants, both Asian, were making the rounds of the large living room, serving drinks and canapés to the two dozen or so guests dressed in tuxedos and suits, evening gowns and expensive-looking dresses. DeWitt grabbed two glasses as one of the trays passed.

"Hey, Rosie, don't you want a drink?" Dick asked as he took a guzzle first from one glass and then the other. "I can get one of these chicks to bring you one."

"Not yet. You see that man with the toupee across the room? He's an old friend that I have to say hello to. Why don't you use your charm and meet some of the count's guests? A few of them are quite interesting and who knows if any need rice?"

Before he could decide whom to charm, Dick felt a hand on his arm. "Did your girlfriend take a powder, mister, or is she just off to powdering her nose?"

DeWitt turned and found himself face-to-face with a pug-nosed, freckled-faced redhead who could have passed for Miss Kansas or Miss Nebraska or Miss Middle America. Unlike the Kraut's other female guests—Rosie excepted—she was not, he concluded, dressed to the tens.

"I don't think we've met, Mr..."

"DeWitt, Dick DeWitt. And what's your nomenclature?" Dick was proud that he had taken a course from Vinny the Vocabulary Man way back when.

The young woman, probably in her middle twenties, frowned. "I'm not sure I have a nomenclature, but my name is Cassie Cassidy."

Feeling empowered by the two drinks he had mostly polished off and by his self-acknowledged charisma, Dick joshed, "Any relation to Hopalong?" His witticism caused him to laugh so hard that he spilled the remainder of his cocktails on the front of a dress that encased an alluring bosom.

"Oops, sorry about that. I guess I got carried away," he apologized as he dabbed at various spots with his moderately soiled handkerchief.

"Stop that, Mr. DeWitt. You're causing a scene and embarrassing me. Besides," she smiled, "we hardly know one another yet."

"There's no time like the present, is there, Cassie my lassie?"

"Well you certainly know how to turn a young girl's head with your words. Tell me, Dick, are you a poet?

Laughing loudly, he nearly spilled the two fresh drinks he had grabbed from one of the passing servers. "Hell no. I sell rice. Just ask that half-Chink who brought me here." Dick looked around the room furtively and leaned closer to Cassie. "I don't just sell rice. I do something else that's a whole lot more important, but I can't tell you because it's a secret."

"Now, Dick, don't be a tease. You shouldn't keep secrets, you naughty man."

"I…" He felt a finger tapping on his shoulder.

"I'm sorry to spoil your fun, Dick, but we have to go now. I have an early morning appointment with my dentist to fix a broken tooth."

Moving closer to Cassie, he whispered, "She should have him fix her nose while he's at it. Maybe he can give her a two-for-one deal."

"Oh, Dick, you're simply terrible, but I'm going to give you my phone number just the same, and I hope I'm not being too forward when I ask for yours."

On their way out, Rosie and Dick said good-bye to their host. "Thank you so much, count, I've had a marvelous time as always."

The count kissed her hand.

"Yeah, me too, count, but you don't need to kiss my hand or anyplace else. And don't forget to keep a stiff upper monocle." Then he handed the count two half-empty glasses, tipped his green fedora, and bid him "Arfweederzane."

"I'm sure the count will never forget you," Rosie said once they were outside.

"You're just saying that to flatter me, Rosie, but a lot of people have said that they'd never forget me. I have that je ne sais squat, I guess."

"You can say that again, Dick."

"I have that je ne sais squat."

Silence prevailed during the trip back.

"We're back to your place, big boy. Stop snoring, wake up, and get out. By the way, a word to the wise. Watch out for that hussy with the red hair, freckles, and pug nose. She's bad news."

Chapter 12

"Has the time come for me to dispose of this pestilent Dick DeWitt, Ichiban? Please say yes."

"I must say no, loyal servant. Not yet. Understand that I would like to place him in a large lobster net and slowly submerge the net into boiling water. Then I would like to peel what remains of his flesh and feed it to hungry pigs, but not before plucking out his round eyes and serving them on a platter of egg foo yung."

"Do you hate him, Ichiban?"

"Yes, and I swear by our Emperor and all our people, that vengeance will be mine."

Chapter 13

DeWitt liked to play it cool. He didn't want dames to think that he was in hot pursuit of them, and so he waited to call Cassie an hour after he awoke the next morning. He walked unsteadily downstairs, his hangover from the party shrieking "I told you so." After tripping over a cat or two on the way to the phone, he dialed his new acquaintance. No answer. She's probably at work, he told himself. Yeah, that's probably it since it's 10:30.

The two Chow ladies and their two Mah Jongg friends were at it as usual, screaming in Chinese and flinging tiles on the board.

"Mrs. Chow?"

"What you want, soldier boy? Can't you see we busy?"

"Sorry, but just in case I get a call, be sure to get the caller's number. Okay."

"Sure okay. You think I no can read or write?" Lotus Blossom continued to give priority to the Mah Jongg board, but added, "Your boss call and say come over chop-chop."

"When was this?… WHEN WAS THIS?" Mrs. Chow.

"No need to shout, soldier boy. He call only a couple of hours ago."

A wave of nausea began to gather in DeWitt, a combination of the previous evening's heroic drinking and the current fear of the colonel's wrath. No time for breakfast. No time for anything but to beat it over to headquarters a.s.a.p.

The aide barely contained a snicker as he told the private that the colonel was fuming. "He frequently fumes anyway, but when he's kept waiting… soldier, I wouldn't want to be in your clodhoppers."

After knocking on the door and receiving a gruff command to come in, De-Witt saluted. "Good morning, sir."

"Oh, is it still morning, private? I guess my watch is slower… almost as slow as you!"

"Sorry, sir."

"Tell me, soldier, have you ever thought of hara-kiri?"

DeWitt pondered for a moment. "A few times, sir. But I find myself thinking more often of Roy Rogers, Gene Autry, and Hopalong Cassidy, and sometimes even of William S. Hart."

A look that mixed disbelief with anger crossed the colonel's face. "No, soldier, I wasn't speaking of the cowboy actor Harry Carey, I was referring to the Japanese custom by which a person who feels dishonored attempts to regain face, so to speak, by plunging a sword or dagger into his entrails."

"I bet that hurts a lot."

"You betcha. I'm certain it hurts a lot, and that's why I asked if you had ever contemplated it."

"No, and I wouldn't want to. When the time comes for the Grim Raper to fetch me, I'd like to be lying in bed with some cutie and a bottle of Jack Daniel's. Have you ever thought of how you'd like to kick the old bucket, sir?"

"Why, yes, but not before I kicked some ass."

"Really? They seem like such innocent animals. Why, if I may ask, would you want to do that. Has an ass ever caused you any problems?"

"You couldn't believe how much," the colonel sighed. "All right, DeWitt, enough of this bullshit. Let's get down to business now that you've decided to pay me a visit.

You may or may not be aware of it—and I'd bet your life that you're not—the military has big plans for building planes for both the Army and Navy to go after those Jap bastards. This, of course, invites spying and sabotage, and we need clever, intelligent, committed people to combat this. Unfortunately, most of them are currently overseas fighting the enemy or sitting on their collective rear ends behind desks brainstorming in Washington. So we don't have much to choose from, but we do have you.

Now here's what you're going to do, DeWitt. Los Angeles has a number of companies that have or will have received government contracts to produce aircraft and roll them out as quickly as possible. I want you, soldier, to hang around some of them and keep on the qui vive for those who want to throw a wrench into the works. Any questions so far?"

"Just a couple, sir. I've never been on the qui vive and, frankly, I don't know where it's located. And as for those wrenches you mentioned, would you happen to have a list of what kinds they are?"

The colonel looked at the ceiling and could be heard questioning if President Roosevelt might consider an exchange of personnel with the Japanese. Not many. Maybe only one.

"Soldier, get yourself out of my office on the double. My aide has a list of instructions for you. Be here promptly—and I do mean promptly—tomorrow morning at 7:00. There'll be someone in front of the building with a car. We're also giving you a .45 automatic. As a rule, only officers carry side arms, but the brass has made exceptions for those on special assignments, especially when they can be dangerous or even fatal." The expression on the colonel's face suddenly changed. "And do be careful with the .45. We don't want you hurting yourself, do we?"

Leaving on the double, DeWitt nearly knocked over the aide, who had his ear to the keyhole. "You know, I didn't know if the colonel actually cared for me, but I can tell now that he's looking out for my well-being. He's quite a guy."

The aide went to a desk and fetched a 9'x12' clasp envelope as well as a small cloth sack that, he said, contained the .45 side arm. "And private, be plenty careful with the weapon. Remember the Army saying, 'You're only as good as your gun.' The colonel would be mighty upset if anything ever happened to the gun. One more thing. I wouldn't be so sure that the colonel thinks you're the cat's meow. If you don't come up with something concrete about spies and saboteurs pretty soon, it will be off to the Pacific for you."

The aide's warning darkened DeWitt's mood. That evening he did what he had done often in the past: he called his pal Polish Phil.

"How are they hanging, buddy boy?"

"They're still hanging, Phil, but I'm afraid my boss might cut them off if I don't find myself a few enemy Japs. Can you think of something?"

The Polack told his friend that he would give the matter some thought and would get back to him.

Twenty-four hours later DeWitt was listening to "The Shadow" on the Chow's radio when the phone rang, interrupting Lotus Blossom's game of solitaire, at which she was mercilessly cheating. "Hey, soldier boy, it's for you."

"Evening, Dick. I've been thinking about your problem and making a few phone calls. There's this former NYPD cop who's now living in Pasadena. His name is Frankie Fusilli, but most of us called him "Itchy Fingers" when he was on the force. He was one tough son of a bitch, but maybe a little bit too tough. He got fired without getting his full pension over a matter of his handling of crime scenes. Almost went on trial, but me and a few other guys pulled a couple of strings, and… well, you know how those things go."

"What exactly did he do, Phil, to get into so much trouble?"

"If you must know, he killed three lousy perps during three separate stake-outs. What really twisted the D.A.'s jockey shorts into knots was that these perps all took it in the back." Phil chuckled. "You didn't want to turn your back on Frankie, if you were looking forward to another hot meal, hot broad, and long, hot piss. But whatever faults he had—if you want to call them faults—he was the sort of guy who got the job done, and if you need to find a Jap bastard or two, he just might be able to help you."

DeWitt took Frankie Fusilli's telephone number, thanked Phil, and promised to keep him informed.

Chapter 14

"Whoever it is, it better be good," said a groggy Itchy Fingers. "You know what time it is?"

"It's 10:15 a.m., Mr. Fusilli. My name is DeWitt, Dick DeWitt, and I'm good friends with Phil Mazurki, who told me to give you a ring."

"You're friends with the Polack, eh? Well, then you can call me anytime day or night. I owe the old bastard big time. So what can I do for you, chum?"

After listening to DeWitt briefly state his problem, Fusilli suggested a late lunch. He would pick him up where he was boarding around 1:00. They would find a place to eat, get to know one another, and hammer out a plan of action.

"Sorry, DeWitt, the traffic is becoming a royal pain in the butt," offered Fusilli, who arrived half an hour later than anticipated. "Know a greasy spoon around here for lunch?

Sammy Burpp was sitting behind the cash register when they arrived. "Hey, Mr. DeWitt, long time no see. You been sick, or you been too busy selling rice?

Fusilli did a double take and was about to ask Burpp what he was talking about.

"No such luck, Sammy," DeWitt quickly answered. "I've been making a lot of calls and visits, and now I've even got my associate, Mr. Fusilli, to help with the sales."

Don't worry, Mr. DeWitt, this year's Chinese New Year sign says that all will be okay, number one, good for everything. Meanwhile we fix you good lunch. Ping Pong will bring you menu."

Fusilli did another double take just as his companion was taking him by the elbow and leading him to a table at the rear of the diner.

Ping Pong ambled over to the table, dropped two menus, grunted, and ambled away. After the two men had decided, DeWitt motioned to the waitress that they were ready to order. By the time Ping Pong arrived, they were more than ready. Fusilli asked for chop suey; DeWitt asked for a cheeseburger smothered with plenty of mayonnaise. Before their lunch came nearly a half an hour later and while they were wolfing it down, DeWitt gave the retired cop the skinny.

"I'm best at giving guys a going over—you know, using my fists or a good old-fashioned knuckle-duster—but I also am good at nosing around. I'll tell you, DeWitt, let me do some snooping and get back to you. I'm all set for cash right now and have some time on my hands. And by the way, do you need a heater? I got a few of them and would be happy to loan you one should you find yourself in need. Wouldn't mind plugging a few Nips myself. Would you?

The former gumshoe thanked the former cop but informed him that the Army had recently supplied him with a rod. DeWitt made a feeble gesture to pick up the check, but Fusilli insisted that this one was on him. "You're a friend of the Polack, and I owe him." DeWitt didn't quibble.

Possessing no leads and a limited imagination, DeWitt spent the next few days passively waiting for Fusilli to call. But he wasted no time in phoning Cassie Cassidy and inviting her for a night on the town. Cassie, dressed in classy evening wear, seemed none too pleased when he parked the car in front of the Brookdale Cafeteria. "Ever been to this joint?" he asked. "They serve really swell chow here. It's a pain in the fanny to have to stand in line, but if you push and shove the way we New Yorkers do, you'll manage real nice."

Cassie assured him that all would be fine and apologized profusely as she stepped on his sneakers. "I guess I got caught up in the bright lights and ex-citement of it all," she explained.

Business was brisk in the cafeteria at this peak hour, and DeWitt had all he could do to shoulder and elbow Chrissie and himself to the front of the line. A few people complained, especially when the gumshoe gave them the bird; more noted how overdressed Chrissie was.

The cafeteria offered a variety of food, as DeWitt had promised. To convince Chrissie of the wisdom of his choice of an excellent place to dine, he offered to share his main dish of hash mixed with tuna fish and surmounted by a dill pickle and chopped onions. Chagrined when she excused herself to find a bathroom, he figured it wasn't worth the effort to repeat his overture.

Having promised a night on the town, DeWitt suggested that a movie would be in order. "There's a great one playing not far from you. I hope you haven't seen *Pinocchio* yet. I keep missing it, and I'm dying to see it."

Chrissie politely declined on grounds that she was allergic to men who had long noses and lied. "How about a drink instead?" she queried.

DeWitt stopped rubbing his nose and quickly agreed. I guess Chrissie has the hots for me, he told himself.

The small bar that Chrissie suggested was only a remove from her apartment, a fact that further convinced the gumshoe of Chrissie's regard for him. A drink or two, back to her place, and who knows?

One drink became two, two became three. This dame can keep up with me, he told himself. He was wrong. By the fourth drink he admitted that she could go further.

"Come on, handsome," she cooed, "stop handing me all this crap about selling rice. I know, and you know, that you couldn't sell a drink to an Irishman on St. Paddy's day. So tell little Cassie what exactly you are doing here in the City of Angels."

DeWitt giggled. "Cassie, you hard-drinking, gorgeous, woman, I'd like to tell you, but it's a great big cigarette… I mean it's a great big secret and Uncle Sam wouldn't want me to tell anyone, even you. See what I mean? All I can say is that our Uncle needs my help in keeping an eye on the enemy. Got it? But mum's the word. Loose ships sink loose slips, they say, and I don't want to be responsible for any loose slips."

"I hear you loud and clear, Dick sweetie. Now I think we'd better call it a night. I don't know about you, but I got a full schedule tomorrow."

DeWitt paid the check and staggered to the door, arm in arm with Cassie. He couldn't remember where he had parked the car, but she did and reminded him of where she lived.

"Can I come upstairs?"

"Honey, you need to go home tonight. Maybe another time." She pecked him on the cheek and told him to drive carefully and sell a ton of rice.

"So long, Hopalong. See you real soon I hope." Five hours later DeWitt was still sleeping in his car when a cop banged on the window and told him to get moving.

Two days later, his hangover scarcely a thing of the past, DeWitt went to the colonel's office in order to lie about making progress. Telling him about Fusilli was out of the question, as was recounting his date with Cassie Cassidy. He was prepared for the worst but was relieved to learn from the aide that the Colonel was indisposed and couldn't see him. The piercing shrieks coming from his office convinced DeWitt that the colonel was much too ill to see him. "Tell the colonel that I'm making real progress and tell him that I hope he feels better from whatever is ailing him."

"I'm sure he'll be glad to hear it," snickered the aide.

Chapter 15

"You got a call, soldier boy," announced Mrs. Chow.

"Hello? This is DeWitt."

"And this is Fusilli. How are you doing, pal? I got some news for you. You ever run into a Kraut named Count Ulrich Ditter von Puffendorff? Yeah? Well he ain't what he seems. He's no more a count than my Uncle Pasquale, who's probably counting the years he still has to serve in Sing Sing. This supposed count was no war hero, believe me. He got himself cashiered from the German Army and nearly court-martialed. Money he's got, however. He made a ton on the black market after the war and another ton when the German government devalued the reichsmark in 1923. Discretion beat out greed when the authorities began breathing down his neck, and the scumbag fled the country soon thereafter."

"So what's he doing in L.A.?"

"Good question. I haven't found out why he came here or when. But I did learn that he bought a big mansion, even as Hollywood big ones go, and has been passing himself off as a war hero and count ever since. The phony bastard has even been spreading the word that he hates the Nazis as much as those Jew directors like Fritz Lang and Billy Wilder who had to flee Germany. Rumor has it that more than a few guests who attend his posh soirees are pro-Axis and that he himself is not a small fry either. So what do you think? Did I do good or did I do good?"

"I can't believe how good you've done, Frankie. You got a nose like a bloodhound. Now what do we do?"

"What do you mean 'we'? I snooped around like I said I would, but I never promised to get more involved. I risked my life as a New York City cop, and look what the Department did to me. No sir, I did my job."

"But you're a good, one hundred percent American, Frankie. Why don't you be like me? I could have sat at home earning a nice living as one of New York's best private eyes, but, no, I told myself that my Uncle Sam needed me badly, and I was one of the first to enroll. I'd lay my life down gladly for my country because it's the right thing to do."

Fusilli remained silent for a long moment before he acknowledged that De-Witt had stirred something within him. "I admit that I don't have your patriotic fervor, Dick, but you put me to shame. I'm in. First thing is that I want to meet this Count Poof—and he probably is one. Do you think that you can arrange it since you're such good friends?"

"No problem, Frankie. I'll ask this broad I know if she'll take me to the count's place again, and if I can bring you along. She's a good sport and like so many dames I left behind, she's got a soft spot in her heart for me."

DeWitt wasted little time before he phoned Rosie O'Grady. "Hi ya, Rosie. This is Dick DeWitt, and I'm wondering if you can do me a favor. I got a surprise visit from a friend from New York who'd love to see Count Putz's place. I told him how gorgeous it is."

"Funny you should mention the count, Dick. He's having another soiree this Saturday, and I would have invited you, but you and the count didn't seem to get along very well when I took you there."

"Nah, Rosie, I was only joshing with him. I promise to make nice with him this time. What do you say?

Well, if you promise not to embarrass me. By the way, what's your friend's name and what does he do? I'd like to let the count know ahead of time."

"His name is Frank Fusilli and he's a… he's a… rice salesman like me. Swell guy, and he really knows his rice."

"I'm sure he does if you say he does.

DeWitt and Fusilli took the latter's car, a late model red Buick, to the soiree. A servant opened the door and welcomed them. DeWitt spotted their host and took Fusilli to meet him. The count was speaking to a woman wearing a tight-fitting backless dress and whose backside seemed familiar to the gumshoe. "Had any sauerkraut and pig's knuckles lately, count?" DeWitt asked, planning to get the evening off to a good start.

The count managed a forced smile. "Well, well, I see that we have the honor of having the illustrious rice salesman with us again. Welcome. Ah, and I see you've brought a friend along. Whom may I have the pleasure of meeting?"

"This is my pal Frankie Fusilli. Say hello to Count Putzendorff, Frankie."

"Charmed, I'm sure, count. You sure got a swell place here," he said, looking around. "Must have cost you a sweet reichsmark or two."

The count gave a slight cough. "And what do you do, Mr. Fusilli?"

"I'm a retired cop. Hey, DeWitt, you just stepped on my nicely brushed shoes. Did you leave your couth at home?" The light went on in Fusilli's brain, and he added, "Of course that was a long time ago. Now I sell rice to Chinks."

"How odd it seems to have two rice sellers at the same soiree," said a woman sporting a backless dress and turning to smile at the newcomers. "I'll bet they sell tons of rice between them."

"Mr. Fusilli, permit me to introduce Miss Cassie Cassidy. And Cassie, I believe you and Mr. DeWitt met here not long ago."

DeWitt's mouth dropped open. "Ah, Cassie, I didn't know you'd be here."

"There are a lot of things you don't know about me, Dick." She laughed. "I'm a mysterious lady, you know."

The count quickly cut in and said that there were other guests whom Cassie needed to meet." Help yourself to the canapés and champagne, gentlemen."

"Who's the babe?" Fusilli asked. "You been holding out on me, pal? Maybe you could let me get to know her better, if you know what I mean."

"Sorry, pal, but I got there first. But you see that dame standing next to the potted palm? You can't miss her. She's got a schnoz like an anteater. Let's go over and you can have a go at her."

"With friends like you, DeWitt..."

"Hi, Rosie, how's life treating you? I want you to meet my friend Frankie from back east."

The trio schmoozed a bit until Frankie said he wanted to socialize and meet some of the other guests. Once he left, Rosie said, "Dick, for your sake, you'd better drop Miss Freckles while you can. I warned you when you met her that she was trouble."

"Come on, Miss Worrywort. Are you jealous that the lady wants to get her hooks into me? Believe me, Rosie, she's no more trouble than you."

"Have it your way then, but don't say I didn't warn you—and twice. Now if you'll excuse me, I see someone I should say hello to."

DeWitt found himself standing alone. A young female server drifted by with a salver laden with champagne. He did not demur: he took two flutes, he told her, to guard against dehydration.

While he was guzzling the second flute of the bubbly, Cassie sauntered over. "Sorry I seemed so abrupt, but I thought it would be rude if I didn't mingle with the count's other partygoers."

DeWitt asked how she had become so friendly with the count. Was there anything between them that he should know about?

"Don't be ridiculous, Dick. He's old enough to be my father. It so happens that he called right out of the blue one day, said that he found me charming, invited me for dinner and dancing at the Mogambo, after which he said it would be a great favor to him if I came to this soiree. Do you think that a young girl from Dubuque who knows so few people in this big city should say no?"

"Well, when you put it that way, I guess I can't complain. But I will complain if you don't let me take you out on another date. A meal at Brookdale's is as good as it gets, and I saw in the newspaper that *Pinocchio* is still playing. What do you say?"

Cassie gave him a big smile. "Okay, you win. I can't say exactly when I'll be free, but give me a ring." With that she kissed him on his cheek and walked away, her hips swaying, her backless dress seemingly cut lower. DeWitt wouldn't need to remind himself to call her. Across the room, Rosie O'Grady grimaced and shook her head.

"Let's blow the joint," a voice whispered in his ear. "I've seen enough."

"So have I, Frankie, so have I."

Chapter 16

"Is it time, Ichiban?"

"Yes, we must act now. The hated enemy, like a wounded lion, begins to regain strength and threaten our plans for a glorious victory. With great shock I have learned that they launched an air strike on Tokyo. Imagine! Now we must move quickly to damage their schedule to build more planes and warships here on the West Coast.

"I am filled with sorrow, Ichiban. Yes, we must strike now. I will do whatever you ask, Ichiban, even if it costs me my life."

"You are a loyal servant of the Emperor and Nippon. Banzai!"

Chapter 17

Two days later the phone in the Chow house rang, interrupting Lotus Blossom's Mah Jongg game with her daughter and their two friends. Lotus yelled up the stairs for her boarder to come down chop chop. "You got some woman on phone who says she must speak with you right away. Urgent, she say. Hey, soldier boy, you get her belly full with child? You sly dog, you."

Still half asleep, DeWitt grabbed the receiver from Lotus Blossom's hand. "Is that you, Cassie?"

"Sorry to disappoint you, Dick, it's Rosie. Listen, Dick, I stopped off at Sammy Burpp's diner this morning. He says he needs to see you about something very big and very secret. Don't come when the diner's open, he said, come about 9:00 this evening. He said he didn't know where you were living or if you had a phone, or he would have contacted you before. Now it's a matter of life and death."

"Did he sound worried, Rosie?"

"Dick, I didn't think you were as dumb as you looked, but now I'm sure. Of course, he sounded worried! Shall I let him know that you'll see him tonight?"

After assuring Rosie that he would meet with Burpp, DeWitt decided that he should report this and the recent soiree at Count Puffendorff's to the colonel. I don't know what Burpp has in mind, he told himself, but it must be pretty important for him to stay late at the diner.

The colonel forced DeWitt to cool his heels for forty-five minutes before yelling to his aide to let him in.

"Make it quick, soldier. There's a war on, which you might or might not be aware of, and I've got plenty on my plate."

DeWitt made no mention that he didn't see a plate on the colonel's desk. 'Sir, I've got news to report."

The colonel pushed back his chair and gave DeWitt a hard look. "It better be good."

"I'm not sure if it's good or bad news, but it's news."

"DeWitt, I just want to hear the news, good or bad," the colonel barked, "now get on with it."

"Yes, sir. Recently I've met a certain German count who may be a phoney. His name is Putzendorff, or something like that. Nothing definite yet, but I'm keeping my eye on him.

"The second bit of news concerns a call I received earlier today. There's this guy, Sammy Burpp, who wants to meet with me tonight. Says it's very important."

"If he's the Chinaman who runs a diner not far from here, I've had lunch at his place. I used to frequent his greasy spoon more often, but it took too damn long to get served. I wonder if he ever got rid of that waitress. She was slower than frozen molasses.

"Okay, soldier, let me know what's doing with Burpp and let me know something more definite about the Kraut. Dismissed."

DeWitt had a lot of thinking to do before his meeting with Burpp. Why does he want to meet, he kept asking himself, and why is it so hush-hush? By late afternoon, having drawn upon his native intelligence and long experience as a private investigator, he reached a conclusion: Burpp wanted him to be the first to know that he was firing Ping Pong.

This took care of two other questions that had been befuddling him. First, should he contact Fuselli about tonight's rendezvous at the Chinese-American diner? Secondly, should he bring along the gun that the Army had provided? No and no. Fuselli was probably busy checking out Count Putz. Besides, I'm able to take care of myself if need be. That led into the second question. DeWitt liked the feel of a gun, the smell of one, the assurance that he could shot himself out of trouble, although that had never happened before. Furthermore, the gun he had in mind was his alter ego, the Smith & Wesson .32 that he had entrusted to his secretary, Ditzy Dotty, while he was serving Uncle Sam. The .45 Colt that the Army had recently given him to carry was too new, too… well, just not his type of side arm.

Anxious to get started on what could prove an interesting adventure, he had one last pick-me-upper from his stash of booze before leaving his room. He waved to Low Fat, who was sitting in the living room listening to some tinny music, and oddly still wearing his policeman's uniform. "What's the matter, Low Fat, they make you wear your uniform off duty, too?"

Low Fat laughed. "No, Dick, I drew double shift today and have to go back on the beat after I grab some grub and relax a bit. These double shifts are ball busters, but a job's a job. Right? DeWitt nodded in sympathy and wished Chow a quiet, uneventful evening.

He wasn't truly hungry but wasn't going to meet with Burpp on an empty stomach. He strolled to Luigi's, an Italian restaurant near Union Station. The food was good there, he knew from experience, the service friendly. The walk from home hadn't much increased his appetite, so he limited himself to an order of eggplant parmesan and a side dish piled high with spaghetti. He poured ketchup liberally over both. Needing to have a clear mind when he met Burpp, he limited himself to two glasses of Chianti. For dessert, he polished off a piece of apple pie and a scoop of Tortoni ice cream.

It was nearly dark when he left the restaurant. The temperature had dropped several degrees, the wind had picked up, scattering debris helter-skelter and causing DeWitt to hold tight to his fedora.

At 8:55 DeWitt reached the diner, whose door bore the sign "Closed," both in English and Chinese. He knocked. Then he knocked harder. It was nearly pitch black inside, without a single light and with all blinds drawn. "Sammy," he yelled, "it's me, Dick Dewitt." He could hear someone banging into a table.

"Hold horse, Mr. DeWitt, I'm coming."

Burpp opened the door. DeWitt could see by what remained of the daylight outdoors that Sammy looked scared, real scared. "What's the matter, pal?"

The diner's owner grabbed him hard by the elbow and dragged him inside. Then he peered out the door and relocked it. "It's terrible, Mr. DeWitt, and I'm scared like crazy. We go in back room to make sure no one see us from street. Watch step, please."

DeWitt nearly fell over a chair that had not been pushed under the table, then barked his shin on a second one. Finally the two men reached the back room. Burpp groped for the light switch that barely illuminated the room with a solitary 40-watt bulb. The room served as storage for boxed and canned food, and few bags of dry food, all bearing Chinese script. A refrigerator stood next to a good-sized safe, in front of which was a desk with chair. Nothing unusual here, the gumshoe deduced.

"So why the secrecy, Sammy? What's going on that we have to talk in the back room of a darkened diner?"

"You're about to find out, Dick." The voice was not Burpp's, unless he was trying out a falsetto one.

DeWitt wheeled around and saw… Rosie O'Grady. She looked the same except for the gun she was holding in her right hand.

"What's this all about, Rosie? Is this some kind of joke? If so, I'm not laughing. Now why don't you give the gat to me before someone gets hurt." He took a step toward her but backed away when she cocked the trigger.

"Good boy, Dick. We wouldn't want anyone to get hurt, at least not yet."

"Who is this 'anyone,' Rosie?"

"Can't you guess, Dick? It's not me, and it's not Sammy, so who's left, or can't you figure it out? And while you're doing the math, Sammy is going to pat you down just in case you brought along a little something for protection." She nodded toward Sammy, who frisked the stunned gumshoe.

"He's clean, Ichiban."

"Ichiban? What the hell is that?"

The word roughly means "Number One" in my native tongue, which is Japanese. It's a sign of respect, and my friend here owes me a lot of that, don't you Sammy?"

"Yes, Ichiban."

DeWitt looked quizzically at Sammy and asked why he owed Rosie respect. The owner of the diner looked down at his shoes and remained silent.

"It's a little matter of threatening harm to him and his family, and burning down his home and business. Wouldn't that induce a lot of respect in you, Dick?"

"Rosie, I'm going to ask you something, and I hope that you give me an honest answer. Are you working for Uncle Sam or the Japs?"

Even Sammy left off looking at his shoes to enjoy a hearty laugh.

"Yes, Dick, since you're not going to be able to tell anyone, I am a Japanese spy, and proud of it. I have been in communication with my government ever since that glorious day, December 7, 1941, the day that will go down in fame. I work with other spies, I recruit others for spying, and I send to Tokyo all the information on American military plans and war materiel that I can lay my busy yellow hands on—as you racist Americans would put it. We shall win this war, but even should we not, I would gladly lay down my life for emperor and country."

"You won't get away with this, you lousy Nip."

"Want to bet? Come on, Sammy, let's take DeWitt out the back door, where my car is waiting. We'll put him in the trunk and take him where he won't be found for some time if ever. A fate he well deserves."

"Hold it right there, O'Grady." Low Fat Chow and Cassie Cassidy came barging through the back room door. "And drop the gun."

Rosie turned her attention from DeWitt to fire on the two intruders, but before she could, a bullet from Low Fat's service revolver smashed into her right shoulder. She went down with a shriek. "You bastards. You'll pay for this. You and the dope who thought I'd fallen for his stupid story that he sold rice. I can spot someone who's undercover, even if he's a dumbbell who doesn't know the first thing about going undercover. I should have plugged him the first time I laid eyes on his ugly kisser," she snarled.

"I'll take the Jap's gun," Low Fat said to Cassie. "You keep an eye on the Chinese guy."

DeWitt remained in shock. "I can't believe this. Who could have thought that Rosie O'Grady was a spy and traitor?"

"Very few," Cassie said. "But our military intelligence unit had its suspicions, and we've been tailing her and her friends for weeks, even before you arrived on the scene. You were out of the loop, as they say, but you did help to nab the notorious Tokyo Nose, as we call her. Good work, Dick. Now we're going to take her and Mr. Burpp to police headquarters. Later we'll have a go at them at Military Intelligence and see if they'll give us names of other spies and would-be saboteurs. And since we're civilized people, Rose's shoulder will receive medical attention.

"You know, Cassie, I would have believed that if you or Rosie were the spy, you'd have been the one."

"We both are spies, Dick. Only I do it for the U.S. Army. I never wanted you to guess my true identity, not at least while we were trying to ferret out traitors. Same goes for Low Fat and his family. We arranged to have you stay at the Chows because we knew they were completely trustworthy but also that Low Fat, as a policeman, could keep an eye on you and report any developments to us.

Low Fat handcuffed Burpp and Cassie held a gun on Rosie, who could not be handcuffed because of her shoulder. Along with DeWitt, they went out the diner and headed for the police cruiser parked nearby. "We'll be in touch," Rosie assured Dick.

"I guess not, Rosie, except maybe at your trial."

We've plenty of time to get reacquainted, DeWitt. Go to hell, and I'll see you there. And by the way, I have friends who soon, I promise, will speed you there. Sayonara, rice man."

Chapter 18

Two days later DeWitt received a call from the colonel's office ordering him to report the following morning promptly at 9:00. He expected a commendation at the very least for his astute work in apprehending O'Grady and Burpp. What he most desired, however, was a transfer. Not that he didn't like Los Angeles. Far from it. But Rosie's promise of vengeance weighed heavily on him. In fact, it was rarely out of mind during waking hours. I'm not scared, he kept telling himself, though aware of strangers passing on the street and noises, both unfamiliar and not.

"He'll see you now," the aide said, nodding toward the colonel's door.

"Good morning, sir."

"So it would seem, DeWitt. At ease." The colonel finished jotting down some notes and then looked up." I called you here to give orders for your next assignment."

"Yes, sir, I was hoping to be transferred, not of course because I haven't been happy with the way you've treated me, but..."

"Skip the ass-kissing, private. You are to remain where you are. It's not that the Army or I necessarily need you or your services, but my immediate superior insists. Your job will be the same, and you'll continue to reside with the Chows, who I'm sure will be pleased as hell to have your company.

"Now before I dismiss you, let me ask if you know anything more about Count Putzendorff. It seems that someone shot him in the back and killed him yesterday. A single witness heard the shot and the assailant screaming something that sounded like it was Italian. Know anything about this?"

A light flickered in DeWitt's brain, but he pleaded ignorance in the matter.

"No big loss," the colonel said. "We were closing in on him anyway. But it's too bad that I—er, we—can't take the credit for apprehending this Nazi sympathizer. Now we can't question him about those parties he threw and who attended them, as well as other traitors he may have been associating with. Okay, private, let us know if you hear anything we should know. Dismissed."

Outside the weather provided a deliciously warm early June day; inside DeWitt remained the chill of impending death. On his way back to the Chows' he passed Sammy Burpp's diner, which, surprisingly, was open for business. Curious, he entered and saw Ping Pong seated at the cash register. "I'm new boss here. You want menu?"

"The king is dead, long live the king." DeWitt remembered the quote from somewhere, while acknowledging to himself that neither Sammy nor Ping Pong was royalty.

When he returned to the house, he was surprised to see that Lotus Blossom and Feng Shui were not engaged in what seemed their eternal game of Mah Jongg. "Good morning, soldier boy. I have good news and bad news. First the bad news," said Mrs. Chow. "The man we play Mah Jongg with, he plenty sick. But there is good news. We learn that you be with us for long time, so we teach you how to play. You like that, soldier boy?"

DeWitt smiled weakly.

"And soldier boy," Lotus Blossom said as she looked to see that no one was within earshot, "Feng Shui say you plenty cute, specially for a round eye. She have no boyfriend, so you can be her boyfriend. You like that?"

DeWitt offered a second weak smile and headed upstairs for his room, where he found the door unlocked, probably because, with so much on his mind, he had forgotten to lock it. Once inside, he smelled something familiar and unpleasant, and saw several felines sitting on his suitcase. He swore, they purred.

It had been that kind of day. Only later would his gloom lighten when he heard on the radio that the U.S. Navy had won a major battle at Midway and had dealt the Japanese Navy a serious defeat that, in retrospect, reversed the tide of fortune in the Pacific War.

Dick wondered if they would give him his medal now.

Disclaimer

All characters in this novel are fictional with the exception of Lieutenant General John L. DeWitt (1880-1962), who was in charge of the Western Defense Command during World War II. A special act of Congress promoted him to full general in 1954.

Lightning Source UK Ltd.
Milton Keynes UK
UKHW012006051120
372880UK00001B/106